This story is a work of fiction. Names, characters, places, and incidents are fictitious and any similarities to actual persons, locations, or events is coincidental.

ISBN: 978-1-998763-33-7

PLAYING HOOKY

JESSICA GLEASON

Prologue

All at once, it carried her, picked Rosalie up as she was stumbling home from the bar Tuesday night, and whipped her into the side of the building, fracturing her skull in the process, leaving her to bleed out into the cobblestones that lined the town's main drag, a twitching congealing mess. It wasn't the way she expected to go, but it was far kinder than the life she'd lived. Strangling out a last breath, she saw it twisting, gathering fallen leaves and roadside litter into its welcoming fold, and then her spotted vision went dark. Forever.

"Famished," the sound hissing out of my absent mouth, a voice for the voiceless, the void in my stomach aching to be filled. "There, a delicious morsel."

In a whipping swirl of motion, I plucked her from the hard concrete, catching a tipsy Rosalie off guard as she stumbled homeward from the bar, much like she did each Tuesday evening. With a forceful shove, I hurled her against the unyielding facade of the building, fracturing her skull in the process. With the echo of a snicker, I whirled away, leaving her to bleed out into the cobblestones that lined the town's main drag, sticky bits of viscera clinging to her face as she twitched there on the ground, her own fluids congealing around her. She was rough, aging before her time, likely the result of a hard-lived life of drinking and casual drug use. It wasn't as violent or satisfying as I'd hoped, instead giving her a much gentler end to her sad, wasted life. But, as her final breaths came out as strangled rasps, she beheld my form, eyes going wide as I beckoned her into my amorphous harsh embrace along with fallen leaves and roadside litter, claiming her as my first. Her heart slowed and stilled before she was enveloped in darkness. Forever.

Chapter One

Opening the door of the spartan auditorium, Professor Micah Spaulding, doctor of abstract art, sighed. "I hate it here," he proclaimed, "seriously, this town is the worst." He'd be more at home amid the high concrete skyscrapers of a vibrant city, one with a burgeoning nightlife, but the teaching jobs were all in the rural rolling hills. So, he was stuck, stifled by acres of corn fields and nestled in a safe, boring pastoral Midwestern community.

Ryan, his scruffy, rakishly handsome science professor buddy, yawned and eyed Micah suspiciously. "What is it this time, Micah? Do tell."

"They don't even have Tito's here." He

gestured wildly, seeming overly devastated at the minor inconvenience. "Who doesn't have Tito's? What kind of suburban hell is this?"

"The vodka? Here, where? This bar or the whole town? Why do you even care, man? Vodka is vodka. Want me to explain the distilling process?" he asked, eyes alight with glee. "I went on a tour last week and got to talk shop with the guide. It was so cool. They had these retro copper pots, and I even know some trade secrets now. Want to start bootlegging on the side? Well, maybe not bootlegging because it's a little dangerous, and I don't want to go blind accidentally, but we could make beer. That's safe enough. Do you want to know how beer is made?"

"No, pass. Beer is gross. I needs me my vodka. Ugh. I bet there isn't a good bottle of vodka in this whole stupid town. This place is boring as shit. Have you seen the yarn store? Who even goes to a yarn store? How can they possibly still be in business? What year is this?" Micah paused, flipping wispy hair away from his angled face. "Ugh…what am I even supposed to drink?"

"You're being dramatic," Dr. Ryan replied. He enjoyed Micah, mostly, but the guy was 110% all the time, over the top, and he made everything seem like the end of the world. Rolling his eyes, he felt embarrassed by his loud friend's ridiculous outburst. The professors in Ryan's department were odd or nerdy, and they were all pretty regimented. None of them would be noisy and exasperated over something so trivial. Micah was on a whole other plane of existence, vibrant and creative, and very, very dramatic. "Have one rail drink, and you won't even care anymore. I promise. Choke it down, and they'll all start to taste good after that."

Micah paused, eyes bulging, and looked at Ryan. "Rail? Did you just suggest rail? Do I look like a pleb to you?"

"Pleb? Who even talks like that? There's an entire row of goddamn vodka. Pick one, dude."

Micah scoffed before eying the vodka selection, eventually lowering his standards, ordering a fancy-flavored Grey Goose mixed drink while Ryan sipped on his piss water cheap beer. The two men had slipped out of their faculty in-service midday because the keynote speaker was a travesty, and neither could stand sitting in a hot, crowded room, all cramped and uncomfortable in those plastic torture chairs, while being force-fed more admin-chosen drivel. If they were going to waste their time, it may as well be getting a little tipsy in a bar instead. With three hundred people packed into that sweltering auditorium, no one would even notice their absence. The faculty and staff were all too busy texting one another to complain or were prepping for the new semester even to see, and the admin were all sitting and listening intently in the first few rows, the ones with the cushioned seats. It was a bit like feudal England, and the faculty was undoubtedly made up of serfs. Ryan was sure they'd snuck out without notice, and he felt relieved to be somewhere less oppressive, even if his friend was a bit much.

Micah scoffed, "Were you even listening to that speaker? She was a whole ass moron, and that tweed suit she had on was an affront to my senses. Yuck."

"Dude, I never listen to the speakers. They pay those people thousands of dollars to spout utter nonsense at us for a few hours. It's a waste of our time and usually short-sighted or in poor taste. After five minutes of a 'well-to-do' White woman explaining her shock at discovering her students had disadvantages, I tuned out. Duh. Of course, they do. We know this. We live this. And we do the best we can with what we're given. Who thought hiring her to tell stories about the time she learned about student poverty was a good idea? If it took her this long to figure out people are struggling, she isn't qualified to help anyone. Instead of dispensing dated advice, she should probably join the rest of us in the real world. Everyone else should have snuck out, too. They're not getting those hours of life back. Idiots."

"So, you did listen!"

"Not really. I doodled and muttered under my breath, mostly." Ryan shrugged, resigned to the terrible speakers the admin chose, resentful of all the wasted time over the years. After the first couple of keynotes, he learned he could sit there and scribble or write up syllabi for the upcoming semester. No one bothered him. No one cared. The bosses were all sitting up front on their thrones anyway. They'd never look back to acknowledge the peons.

"I hate when they do this shit, pay these people thousands of dollars to poorly explain stuff we already know or, like, sometimes drone on about stuff that has nothing to do with anything we do. Do you remember the dude who made us fill out some Catholic school dropout worksheet on sinners and sinning? Is that shit even legal? Don't we have, like, separation of church and state?"

Ryan shrugged. "I turned the worksheet illustration into the devil. It made me feel better. I hope it ruined someone's day when I handed it in."

"I mean, that's pretty funny. But, still, I don't know why we had some religious zealot lecturing to us. We're a state school."

"Like I said, Micah, it's a waste of fucking

time. Maybe bring an iPad and do some digital painting."

"Ew. Digital. Shudder." Laughing and thinking his friend silly, Micah sat trying to calculate the time he'd wasted at meetings and training over the years, but he gave up after a few seconds. He could have been in the studio creating, but the admin wanted to crush his spirits instead. "Do you think they'll notice we walked out?" Slightly worried about administrative retribution, Micah didn't want any other targets on his back.

"Do you care?"

"I mean, I don't want anyone gossiping about us, and I used both days of my time to go to a music festival last semester," he replied, smiling a nervous smile and showing far too many of his large teeth.

"If anything, they're wishing they were us." Ryan laughed. "But, really, no one's going to snitch even if they do notice we're gone. We scanned in this morning. That's all we really needed to do. We could have probably slunk back to the parking lot right away. They don't pay enough attention to even know who we are. We're just nameless faces."

A stiff wind smacked against the building, slapping sounds mixing with the bar's ambient noise.

"Yikes," Micah said, jumping from his seat, startled by the angry weather outside.

Thankfully, the bar was nestled in an old industrial building, which once served as an ironworks factory. The place had a unique charm to it, with exposed piping and high steel-beamed ceilings. It was probably the safest building in town to weather a storm.

"It's pretty nasty out there," Micah said, noting the noise. "I hope it dies down before we call it a night."

"Yeah, the trees were bending a little on the way here. My car was all over the road. I'm glad we didn't walk. I can't wait for whatever awful weather's coming our way." Bringing the amber bottle to his lips, Ryan tipped the rest of the hoppy fluid down his throat and signaled to the bartender that he'd like another.

"Here ya go," the attractive brunette offered, leaving him an ice-cold beer and a flirtatious wink before heading back to her perch and picking up a dog-eared copy of some dated sci-fi novel. Briefly, Ryan considered chugging his beer so he could call the woman back over and do some flirting himself. Discarding the thought, he grabbed the new beer and took a sip, letting the cool liquid slide down his throat. He wanted to make headway on forgetting the morning's in-service trauma, but he didn't need to get sloppy drunk on a school night. Cold beer, he found, was better than therapy, and it made him a little more courageous, too. *Maybe I'll get up the nerve to flirt back later.*

"I can't believe they waste so much of our time before the new semester starts. Like, we could be relaxing and recharging or, I don't know, getting our classes ready? But, no, tomorrow we've got a whole day of enrichment activities. Who wants that?"

"No one," Ryan grumbled, shuddering at the thought of another essential oil class or *business casual* yoga.

"And it's not like either of us can organize our labs or studios remotely. We have too much to do, and they're not respectful of our time. When do I prep? Late at night? The weekend? They think we belong to them. It's just maddening. I have a two-hour balloon animal workshop in the morning. Balloon animals! I swear to the Lord above, if a clown teaches it, I'm quitting my job. I don't need that kind of negativity in my life." Lost in another tirade, Micah worked himself into a frenzy.

Ryan agreed and nodded.

Pausing to collect himself, Micah tapped his nails on the side of his glass and took a few deep breaths before turning to his friend again. "What'd you sign up for this time?"

"Eh. I didn't. I usually just look at what's left and sign up the morning of, but I think I'm going to call in sick tomorrow. The way we're going, I'll probably feel a little under the weather anyway." He laughed.

Micah chuckled. "A hangover isn't sick."

"It sure feels like sick to me," he began, shrugging, "and I've got sick time to burn. I could use a mental health day. They're always going on about making time for self-care, right? Mental health days are self-care. Learning how to upcycle old jeans is not."

"Well, you may be onto something, man. I couldn't find anything even remotely interesting. I think I rounded out my day with charcuterie board making and the one where they bring in the dogs from the shelter so we can pet them or whatever. How is that suitable use for a workday?"

"Yeah, I already feel sick. I'm not wasting a day on nonsense. I just can't even with their bullshit anymore. Don't get me wrong, I like dogs, but I don't think spending two hours forcibly petting or walking them is doing anyone much good. Well, the dogs probably like it, I suppose."

The two men continued, drinking in the relative comfort of the bar, letting the liquor wash over them, blur things, making the world just a little fuzzy around the edges. They weren't close friends, per se, but being office mates, they'd formed a kind of kinship, a shared misery.

"You know, I don't hear any rain. Just all that thwapping and those shrill shrieks," Micah said. The wind whipped, whistling past the building, unrelenting and violent.

"Well, then, I guess we won't get soaked. Look at that. The day is looking up already." Ryan held up his bottle in a mock salute.

"Hopefully, the storm part holds off. However, I don't think either one of us should leave any time soon. I, for one, cannot walk a straight line to the bathroom, let alone get to my car to drive home."

The guys ordered a selection of fried nonsense: cheese curds, pepper jack cheese-wrapped pickles in wonton shells, and baby corn dogs, something to soak up the booze a little and to complete their trifecta of bad choices.

"This shit is tasty," Micah proclaimed, wiping his filthy hands on a bar napkin halfway through their artery-clogging feast.

"So much better than the institutional sandwich and chips they'd have fed us at work," Ryan agreed while greedily popping another mini corn dog in his mouth. "My insides are going to be wrecked."

The afternoon had given way to early evening, and Ryan and Micah decided it was about time to call it a night. Their feast had tempered the alcohol enough for them to venture home safely. Tuesday wasn't the best time for a bender, and they agreed tomorrow would be a shit show no matter what. Ryan was particularly disappointed because he'd never worked up the nerve to flirt with the cute bartender. He'd made a mental note to come back again soon, thinking he might flirt with her then. But today's chance had passed him by. At this point, he'd wake up regret-filled and hating the world, and he didn't want to sour a potential flirtation by barfing on the woman's shoes. So, leaving was an act of self-preservation.

"Alright, Micah, let's get out of here," Ryan said, zipping up his green jacket and pulling on a gray knit cap.

Micah grabbed his chic coat, slinging it over a shoulder, and stretched before responding, "Fine. Party pooper."

They paid their tab and meandered to the exit, genuinely believing they'd made a wise choice in ducking out of work to have a little fun but not knowing how right they had been to do so.

Once outside, the odd pair had trouble walking in a straight line, their bodies lazily swaying and bumping one another every few feet. They blamed their lack of balance partially on the booze and partially on the wicked current. Their shoulders touched as they stumbled down the sidewalk at the mercy of the devastating wind.

Ryan, shielding his eyes, looked at Micah bewildered. "Fuck, this is nuts. I am not that drunk."

"Yeah, my tiny, shitbox car is not going to be fun to drive tonight!" Micah added, yelling a bit to be heard over the sound of the wind. "It's a tiny little shitbox. Can't wait to white knuckle it back to my place."

"Maybe we shouldn't be driving! This feels unsafe! Turn back and wait it out?"

"Eh, we drive home through whiteout snowstorms! We'll probably be fine!" Ryan replied, wanting to get home, take off his khakis, and rest in front of his television in just a pair of boxers and his fuzzy robe.

"I guess, but this feels like a tornado! I wouldn't be surprised if a cow flew by!"

"There'd be a siren!" Ryan said, gesturing wildly at his friend, but being tamped down by the roaring winds instead. His pantomime was more confusing than helpful.

"Maybe we wouldn't hear it?"

The two made slow work of walking down the block, not noticing the outstretched hand reaching from behind the mailbox, frozen in its final configuration. Neither did they see the window of the artisanal cheese shop had been shattered, blown into the store, shards of glass embedded in the still cooling customers and employees who'd been inside the shop; the whole place was littered with battered corpses and drying pools of congealed blood. The once neat niche storefronts were marred with blood spatter and the stink of bloating corpses.

As they rounded the corner near the town bank, catching a foul stench on the harsh winds, the men found themselves momentarily shielded from the winds while pinched between the large brick building and a parked tourist trolley from a nearby resort. Slowing a moment to sooth their burning leg muscles, Micah finally noticed something was amiss after nearly tripping over a woman, skull shattered, dead, and lying in a sticky pool of her own blood.

"Oh. My. God!" Micah squealed, rushing over to Ryan's side, latching onto his arm like a little child.

"What the hell, man? What are you doing?" Ryan yelled, trying to shake off his clingy coworker. "Let go!"

Micah, face contorted into a horrific grimace, screamed, "She's dead!"

"Who's dead? Get off me! Why are you being dramatic again?" Ryan pried Micah's fingers from his arm.

Micah grabbed Ryan's head and swiveled it to

where he'd seen the dead woman. "Her, that speaker we ditched out on. I'd know that disgusting tweed suit anywhere. She's fucking dead."

"Holy shit." Ryan scrambled backward a few steps, shocked and unsure how to react. He'd never seen a dead body before, except the cadaver from grad school.

"I. Told. You. At least no one else will have to listen to her drivel anymore," Micah said.

"Micah, dude, not cool."

Horrified, Micah's eyes went wide. "Oh. I said the inside part out loud again, didn't I?"

Chapter Two

Inspecting the keynote speaker's corpse a little closer, they decided it looked like her limbs had been broken as if she'd been dropped from high up. She'd been jangled around in some way or just busted up really bad. Though, for someone with a bone sticking through the skin, there was remarkably little blood. She'd died in some inexplicably horrific manner, that much was certain, and her body was just lying there pinned to the brick wall of the bakery's storefront by the powerful winds. Not knowing what to do, both men looked to one another for guidance.

"You're the science guy. Can't you science?"

Micah asked.

"I'm not like a forensics scientist!" he yelled, trying to be heard over the rush of the winds. After taking a few deep breaths, Ryan continued, "I think we need to go back to the bar! It's closer! Don't touch her; I'm not comfortable lingering here…"

The wind howled violently around them, sending little pebbles into their skin and causing a torrent of minor pain to bloom across any exposed flesh. Micah struggled into his jacket before they began moving once again.

They turned, attempting to hurry but fighting against the violent pressure seemingly pushing in on them from all directions. The wind was almost squeezing them like old, used-up toothpaste tubes. It was everywhere at once, confusing, as it whipped Micah's hair to-and-fro.

"I'm telling you. Something's wrong here," Micah said, his panic seeming more and more reasonable as time passed. "These are monster winds. Deadly monster winds."

Ryan shot a hand out in front of him, wanting to feel where the wind was coming from. Shockingly, his outstretched arm whipped behind him, straining the joint and causing a numb sensation to shoot from his armpit to his fingertips. "What the fuck?" he screeched, befuddled and slightly afraid as he grabbed his wretched arm, cradling it against his body for safety. "This is no monster, but it's wicked. That's for sure. Let's hurry!" His skin prickled into gooseflesh as his body reacted to the threat of being stuck in the unnatural winds.

It was near impossible to run, but before long, they'd made it back to the bar, a little disheveled and out of breath. Opening the doors was more difficult than prying open a long-sealed mason jar; a wind-induced vacuum attempted to keep them from entering, from finding relative safety. The wind seemed to mock them as it jostled them about, denying them entry. But the two professors pooled their strength and pried the door open with a satisfying sucking pop.

Ryan's hands were red and raw from the effort, "Thank goodness," he said before wiping sweat from his forehead, worn down from the strain.

"What do we do now?'' Micah asked, bracing himself against the now-closed door.

"I think we probably call the police and tell them what we saw?"

"Okay. Okay. Let's go sit down at the bar. You call, and I'll tell that bartender we need some help or something. I hope she's got some kind of weapon back there. "

"I don't know if we need to worry her right now," Ryan replied, pragmatic and not wanting to be an alarmist. This was different from the introduction he'd hoped to have with the pretty bartender in that moment of near flirtation that'd passed between them. "There aren't too many people here, but there's no use riling them up until we need to."

Ryan looked around to assess their environment. For a dive bar, the place was fairly quiet. An older man sat near a wall covered in vintage license plates. He didn't seem terribly drunk or unruly, but the way he sucked down his entire stein in a single pull, while impressive, did give Ryan some cause for concern. A younger duo was animatedly talking while seated in two comfortable looking chairs near the corner of the bar. Ryan couldn't tell if they were an excited young couple wildly gesturing as they planned a date night or if they were related in some way and chiding one another as siblings do. The only real wild card was the unkempt woman near the jukebox screeching an off-key rendition of "Cat Scratch Fever" while thrashing her arms in all directions and awkwardly jerking about to the song.

"Yeah, but don't you think she'd want to take maybe some safety precautions like locking the door or something?"

"Sure. Okay. Fine. I'm going to the bathroom

to make the call."

Ryan attempted to call the police. But when he unlocked the screen, he found his cell phone had no service. He moved to several spots in the bar, but each call attempt resulted only in a long beep and the click of a hangup. So, he sidled up near Micah whose arms flailed animatedly, dramatically as he recounted the last several minutes for the bartender, waiting for a break in the conversation.

"Uh, hey, so my phone has no service. Does anyone else want to give it a go? We should probably contact the cops sooner rather than later, yeah?"

Both Micah and the bartender, Jade, whipped out their phones only to find that they, too, lacked service.

"Nope," Jade added.

Micah held his phone up, showing the X where his bars should be. "Same here."

Ryan tugged at his beard for a moment. "Um, well, does the bar have a landline? Do those work the same way?"

"They don't, and we do. I'll make the call." Jade walked off and out of view, presumably to a back office.

Turning to Micah, Ryan felt lost. "What do we do if no one gets through the emergency services?"

"I don't know, maybe we sit down and have a

drink or three. There are ways to distract ourselves while we're here."

Looking around, Ryan did see how playing darts or pool might help them calm down and pass the time.

Ryan looked to Jade as she returned to the bar. "No luck?" His buzz had worn off, leaving only fear and concern.

"Well, it works, but no one answered," she said, seeming both annoyed and a little disturbed.

"Wait, no one answered what?" Micah asked.

"Nine-one-one."

His eyes bulged. "No one answered nine-one-one? What the hell? Is that even a thing?"

"It is right now. I'll try again in a few minutes." She shrugged. "Maybe their lines are jammed with wind-related calls."

Ryan and Micah, exchanged another worried glance. They couldn't leave. They couldn't contact help. They were at a loss. Jade seemed much calmer, metered, and even, but she hadn't almost fallen over a bloody corpse.

"Okay, maybe we should step outside and see if there's anyone on patrol yet?" Ryan, not wanting to seem a coward, offered. He knew the walking cops would patrol once night had fully taken hold. They always did, pacing the streets eager to ticket under-agers and drunks on bicycles.

"Outside? With the psycho killer? No thanks," Micah replied, his shrill voice increasing in volume.

"Well, what if the killer came in here? What if they're already inside?" Ryan asked. He was pragmatic and knew that, realistically, the killer could have been in the bar for hours. They hadn't stopped to check the dead lady to see if she was still warm or if rigor had set in. She could have been there for hours; anything was possible.

"What? What the fuck? Why would you say that? Is nothing sacred? I cannot deal with more trauma. If I wake up with a stress zit tomorrow, I'm blaming you." Micah furrowed his brow and felt around for the hint of a breakout before glaring at his friend.

"I'm just saying, Micah. What if? We don't know shit. We have to think this through."

Stunned, Micah considered his colleague's words. "Fine, we can look for the cops outside, but after five minutes, I'm out. I'm not into being the hero."

"Fair."

The two left Jade in charge of trying the police again and made their way outside to look for some kind of help. The wind was still strong, oppressive even, and it was hard to look up and out without needing to blink the grit from their eyes constantly.

Sight cast slightly down, the two began to struggle along the sidewalk again.

"This is bizarre. Like, I think we're inside a tornado. I mean…not us specifically, but the whole damn block or something. I bet this is what it sounds like inside a vacuum, you know?" Micah said, rambling nervously. He looked down at the tiny red welts he'd earned on his last trip out. He wasn't the type to rush into danger, preferring to watch from the sidelines and gossip about it later instead.

"Try not to worry too much. Weather happens. It's just extra windy." Stopping dead, Ryan looked over to Micah, thoughts interrupted.

"What's wrong? What is it? Do you see something?"

Shakily, Ryan replied, "I do."

"Well, tell me! I'm already terrified." Micah latched onto Ryan's arm again, ghost-white and shivering, "I'm not built for this kind of stress."

Without explanation, Ryan spit out a firm command: "Turn around or start backing up. We need to go back to the bar now." He shook Micah loose, but put a protective arm out across Micah's chest and pushed him backward toward the door.

"Why?"

"Look across the street," Ryan replied, pointing.

"Is that a hand?" Micah asked.

"Probably. Look up and over. To the left a little."

Micah's jaw dropped, this time out of legitimate fright and not because of some imagined crisis. "What the hell? What is that? Are they…"

Ryan finished the question: "Dead. Real dead."

The building across the way was decorated with unfortunate people, pinned to the wall, hanging by strips of dead flesh. Their skin, a sallow tone, an indicator that no life was left in their dangling bodies. None of them struggled or twitched any longer, which was to their benefit, as some where shredded by broken glass, the remnants of their blood dripping down on to the pavement. Others had missing jaws, their mouths open in final scream configurations and some were ripped open, slit across the belly with their ropey intestines bulging and spilling out of their bloating bodies. The only movement was wind-induced thwapping of limbs and the strikingly harsh ripping of hair from their flesh as their exposed bodies were violated by the inclement weather.

"Get going. Back inside, now."

Neither man had noticed the broken window of the cheese shop nor the carnage inside, but bodies dangling from an abandoned storefront, and a dead mailman were enough to send them flailing toward the safety of the bar once again.

"Wait," Micah grabbed Ryan's arm firmly, "listen."

"I don't hear anything except the wind." Uncertain of what he was supposed to be hearing, Ryan paused a moment longer in case he'd missed something.

"Exactly."

"Exactly what?"

"What happened to all the shrieking? Why can't we hear people or animals or anything? I don't even hear, like, trash bins rolling down the road. It's just the fucking loud ass wind. Shouldn't there be noise from other buildings? Shouldn't there be people? At least a few? There's nothing. Where did they all go?"

"I...I don't know. Maybe the wind is just drowning out the rest of the noise. We need to get back inside."

"Yeah, but don't you remember all of that screeching and howling from before? We've heard it for hours. If the wind is still here, why can't we hear that anymore? Where did it go? Why did it stop?"

"What are you trying to say?" Ryan began, not understanding Micah's line of thinking, until something terrible dawned on him. "Wait...You don't think..."

"That those were actual screams before? I sure do. Look at those people. Do you feel like they died quietly? I think we were listening to mass murder without realizing it."

"Okay, that's really messed up, but let's get back inside."

Micah nodded and turned back toward the bar. "Wait? Why aren't there any lights? The sun's barely visible. There should be streetlights and shit. Yeah?"

Looking around, the two noted the only lights within view were those outside the bar, the lonely neon sign a beacon in the darkening night.

"Why aren't there any lights except the ones at the bar?" Micah asked.

Ryan scratched his head, still feeling desperate to reach shelter again. "I just don't know. Come on."

Confused and feeling unsafe, they tried running back toward the bar's shelter and relative safety but made slow progress fighting against the wind. Each step felt like slogging through three feet of wet mud and little pebbles snapped hard against their skin as they struggled towards their destination. Upon reaching the door, both men had beads of sweat running down their forehead and into their eyes, the salty sweat stinging as they rapidly blinked trying to clear it from their tear ducts. Ryan tugged at the door but was denied entry, "Help me open this thing. It's stuck."

"Ugh, I wasn't built for manual labor." Despite his whining, Micah grabbed the door and they both yanked. Still, the door held firm as wind whipped hard against it, thwarting their ministrations.

Both men pulled back once more, using their weight as they yanked and the door finally came free with a sucking pop. Ryan and Micah scrambled inside before slamming the door shut behind them.

"No one goes out there," Micah boomed as soon as the door closed behind him. "Lock this door. Barricade the entrance. I don't even know."

The smattering of patrons looked over, a sparse group, expressions of dismay and annoyance crossing their buzzed faces. No one moved, save Jade, who brought her key ring to the entrance and locked both of the entryway doors.

"You heard the man, move the heavy stuff over to the door," Jade ordered.

Cautious glances were exchanged, but the dutiful regulars listened and began pushing pool tables and other furniture across the entryway. The building was heavy stock, and the doorway was its only weakness. The door itself was solid, thick industrial metal. It was probably as close to a fortress as they'd get downtown.

"Listen up, everyone, these two boys have something to say," Jade said, her booming voice noting the seriousness of the situation and commanding attention of the patrons in her establishment. The group looked from Jade to the professors, now seeming more curious and alarmed than they'd been seconds ago.

Ryan and Micah exchanged worried glances once again before Ryan stepped forward to speak. "Um... So, don't go outside. There are bodies everywhere. The cops aren't answering nine-one-one, and the wind seems unnaturally brutal."

No one said much of anything, eyes darting about before finally settling on Jade for confirmation.

"I know this sounds outlandish, but I'm inclined to believe them. There's clearly some kind of storm out there, and we're having trouble reaching emergency services. Something's definitely up."

"So, what do we do now?" a concerned-looking older man asked.

"We wait," Ryan offered.

"Yeah, we wait," Jade said.

Several patrons pulled out their phones, frantically tapping on their bright screens, but finding no connections or answers.

"Shit!" a young man exclaimed.

"No service, I assume," Micah asked.

There were grunts and nods. Everyone was stuck, safe in the bar for now, but stuck. A sense of panic filled the room, but unsure of what else to do, they all settled back into their drinks, gulping greedily, emptying their glasses, and looking to Jade for replacements. She obliged, not charging anyone for the next round.

"Don't worry, folks. The landline is still working and I'm sure the cells will be back up soon. Let's buckle down for now and I'll keep trying the emergency number until we get ahold of some help. Sound good?"

Chapter Three: Earlier on Day One

"Let's all thank Ms. Presswick for her outstanding thoughts on student disadvantage and poverty," the provost called, clapping as the woman exited the stage—she'd captured the necessity for instructors to go beyond the classroom to ensure they were meeting the needs of disadvantaged learners. His stupid faculty was probably learning a ton, and that was all due to him.

The group was primarily silent, rolling their eyes or playing with their electronic devices, save a small group of administrators who were fervently clapping.

"That was really bad," a mousy woman said, leaning close to the mustachioed man beside her, "like epically bad."

"Yeah, she was really out of touch. I can smell the white privilege on her from way back here," his gravelly voice rumbled, full of apathy.

"I bet she had a nanny who tucked her in and read her fairy tales about pretty little girls finding princes every night."

At the front of the room, the next presenter was introduced. "I'd like to welcome Mr. Edwards to the stage now to give an update on benefits," the provost said before exiting and taking his seat in the front row.

"Good morning…or, is it afternoon now?" The man chuckled to himself, looking around, perhaps expecting laughter and smiles, but when no one reacted, he blushed and began perspiring before continuing. "I'm Flip Edwards, your HR manager, and I'm here for the not-so-fun portion of our program. Don't hate me, though; I'm just the messenger." He laughed nervously, sent out like a lamb to slaughter, the school's scapegoat.

Many of the crowd looked up from their devices, sneers on their faces.

"Why do they do this to us right before we start the semester?" Malaysia Johnson, a World History professor, asked no one in particular. Her neighbor,

Benetto Constanza, the lead laboratory technician, leaned over and whispered, "Because they're evil. They get off on this shit."

"As I was saying, we're going to be making some changes around here, and it's important for you to understand the impact this will have on you moving forward," Mr. Edwards began. "After today's meeting, you'll receive an email and an attachment outlining all of these changes. Please make sure to sign and acknowledge it before the start of the new semester. You can send it back to me or to your department's associate, and we'll get you marked off the list."

"Boooooo!" Someone shouted from the back row. "This place is bullshit!" The heckler stood, marching out the door and leaving with a flipped bird, all pomp and circumstance.

"That guy is my hero," Benetto said, not able to contain his warm laughter.

"Oh my God," Malaysia replied, "that was amazing, highlight of my fucking career."

A small chorus of laughter broke out in the room while others averted their eyes. The provost stood, using his hands in a *hushing* motion and yelling for people to calm down so the presentation could continue. "Someone will handle that…incident, but we need to get back to our program, folks. Nothing stops progress! We have a schedule to keep! Mr. Edwards, please continue."

The HR manager, to his credit, was stifling a laugh of his own.

"Maybe the old guy isn't the enemy?" Benetto said, nudging Malaysia's arm. "Who do you think really pulls the strings up there?"

"The Illuminati, probably," she replied, giggling quietly to herself. "Robot overlords—the provost has always looked a little plastic or waxy to me. I bet he's just an android, programmed to smile our way while delivering horrendous news."

Tapping his microphone a few times to send a boom across the auditorium, Mr. Edwards continued. "As I was saying—"

A loud horror movie-quality scream broke out across the room, interrupting Mr. Edwards.

Eyes wide, he covered the mic and looked down at the small group of administrators. "What now?"

The provost motioned for him to continue and then, along with two other men in expensive suits, got up to exit the room.

"Well, isn't today eventful?" Mr. Edwards began, nervously joking. "Sorry for the interruptions, everyone. I really do want to get through this as quickly and painlessly as possible. As you know, the college formed a committee this year to look at our health insurance coverage and to explore alternative options…"

No one was really listening, not after the screaming started. Conversations broke out. Some stood. Many just looked around with wide panicked eyes, frantically looking to-and-fro for a solution.

As Mr. Edwards continued sputtering behind the podium, the three administrators barged back into the room, hands covered in blood, speckles staining their gray suits, and crimson smears across their faces. The provost was no longer metered as he began frantically yelling.

"What the fuck?" Mr. Edwards said, forgetting to cover the microphone. "What's happening out there?"

The provost ran up the steps of the stage, shoving Flip aside. "We need to evacuate. Everyone get up and file out in a quick but orderly fashion."

No one moved.

"What's wrong with you idiots? Get up and move!" the provost spat, his angry face turning red to match the splotches of blood littered about his brow and lips.

The attendees looked to one another for guidance. Three higher-ups, covered in blood, ran into the room, and this guy wanted them to leave. To go out into whatever nightmare they'd encountered?

"Why?"

"What's going on?"

"Tell us, or we're not going anywhere?" Came the bold voice of a Spanish professor.

"Listen, man, there's no time to talk! A man's been turned inside out!"

Wrinkling his brow, the Spanish professor asked, "Inside out?"

"Yes, like someone ripped off his skin and laid it out, leaving him to wretch, his organs exposed. Inside out."

"That's preposterous."

"Does it look like I'm playing 'Señor, whatever your name' is?"

"Even if what you're saying is true, why do I want to race out into that? Shouldn't we lock the doors and call for help or something?"

The provost, clenching his fists and turning a bright shade of beet red, huffed and ran out the door once again, leaving a stunned room of educators and administrative professionals behind.

Some people were whispering, but most hadn't even processed the last few minutes yet. Malaysia grabbed Benetto's arm, cocking her head to the side, beckoning him to follow her.

"Where are we going?" he asked.

"Just follow me," she said, the force evident in

her voice. She'd have made an outstanding middle school teacher, stern and confident, using her tone expertly in a way that no one would dare question.

"Okay, you're the boss."

Malaysia had a fondness for old buildings in the town. She was drawn to them the same way she was drawn to study history, and she knew that this building had an old fallout shelter. She led her friend to the rear of the room, motioning for Annette, a friendly new design instructor, to follow.

Malaysia stopped them at a utility closet. "I think it's in here somewhere."

"What is?" Annette asked.

"You'll see, come on. Let's get in before anyone else sees us." Looking around to make sure no one was paying attention to them, Malaysia beckoned her small group to enter the closet while the coast was clear.

The three piled into the cozy space, closing the door behind them. Malaysia flipped on the light, noticing a hatch below one of the metal shelving units in the corner. "Help me move this, okay?"

Benetto, mustering his strength, pulled at the shelf while the two women pushed. They managed to uncover the hatch, which, while sealed fairly tight, was easy enough to pry open.

"Down we go," Malaysia said, using her arm

to gesture, in a grand flourish, to the hole in the floor.

"We're going in there?" Benetto asked. "Why?"

"Bomb shelter."

"We don't even know what's going on?" Benetto offered.

"So? Best case scenario, we avoid whatever awful thing everyone's freaking out about, right? It's a fallout shelter. This puppy can withstand a lot. We'll be safe, I promise."

Annette and Benetto looked at one another, shrugging in resignation, and followed Malaysia down into the hole. As they descended the ladder into the cool and cavernous room, they never imagined it'd be the last home they'd ever know, nor that they wouldn't see the outside ever again.

—

Once the provost reached the door, letting the wind in once again, his skin was painfully stretched from his face before the unseen force caused it to tear from his musculature. The mad wind whipped around him, ripping flesh until he, too, was a naked mass of bone and muscle, fat and blood. He writhed in agony, falling to the floor as his screams pierced the halls of the small building. Using his arms to shield his more sensitive organs, the provost screamed for help, sloppy fluids leaking and puddling around him. The bright fluorescent lights made his exposed insides gleam like a freshly washed and waxed new car. It was repulsive but also beautiful in the right light. He jerked in agony, unable to move, until his life slipped painfully away.

The auditorium was filled with his final wet, choking screams, which threw the group into a panic. The remaining blood-covered administrators tried to keep order, throwing themselves at the doorway and attempting to keep everyone in the room.

"People, people, we don't think you should leave."

"So, we just wait in here for whatever's out there to get us?"

"I'm sorry, folks, we just don't know anything right now. The sensible thing is to barricade the doors and call for help. We have emergency plans for just this reason. Consider this a lockdown. We need to close and block these doors, get these lights turned off, and then we need to move to the far wall. We've practiced this. Let's get to it."

With no security to speak of, it was almost impossible for two office-dwelling administrators to handle the surging crowd. A swell of people pushed their way forward, closing in on the administrator standing guard at the door.

"Stop! Stop! You're hurting me!"

As the swarm of people shoved forward, the administrator fell to the ground and was trampled to death by the soles of dozens of educators' feet. His poor head caved in with a loud crunch and leaked vital fluids into the industrial carpets, shards of his skull fragmenting and piercing the shoes and feet of educators as they stomped on his pulpy corpse.

Once those pressing to get out had ventured past the threshold filling the halls, the more sensible folks made quick work of kicking the remainder of the administrator's body into the hall and closing the doors once again. They locked and barricaded themselves in. In minutes, the whole building was filled with screams, people thrashing around, and loud thumps hitting the walls. Then came the pounding, people they'd worked with for years begging to get back into the room. But no one moved to help. They couldn't risk it. Those agonizing howls and shrieks went on for nearly a half hour before everything, save the rushing of the wind, went silent again.

"Should we go out there and check the halls?" a mousy woman offered.

"No, no, I don't think we should," came the voice of Mr. Edwards, the lone HR representative still left in the room. "They chose to go out there.

We did not."

"Well, then, what are we supposed to do?" the same woman asked.

"Call for help?"

Everyone grabbed their phones, holding them in the air, looking for service, but no one had any. The small group, about fifteen people, looked at one another, visibly uncertain and terrified.

"What were you going to tell us anyway, Mr. Edwards?" Came the voice of the health and science department's chair, Tawney Reese.

"That hardly seems to matter now. Not at all," he replied.

"Well, what are we supposed to do?" she asked.

One of them had to act as an authority figure.

He paused for a second, then asked, "Does anyone want to fuck?"

"Wait, what did you say? That has to be an HR violation," Tawney replied.

"Sorry, stress makes me horny. It's why I love my job so much," he said, blushing.

There were a few hushed murmurs from the group. They were all stressed and confused and terrified, and, apparently, horny. "You know what," Tawney began, "why the fuck not? Fuck this place." She began unbuttoning her dress shirt, revealing her mismatched puke green granny panties and full coverage tan bra, "So much for being an Ethics professor," she said, as she readied herself for fondling and insertion on school property.

The group laughed at the ridiculousness of what was happening, but everyone in the room embraced the moment. *How often do you get to fuck in the workplace? With the HR manager present, nonetheless.* Their situation was dire, but they may as well enjoy these moments in a pile of panting and rutting flesh. So, they did. The HR manager, surprisingly, was blessed with a large cock that had a favorable curve, becoming a crowd favorite.

"My God," the mousy woman, Martha, squealed, "give me a taste of that bad boy." Her pleasure was the loudest.

Chapter Four

Jade leaned over, her cleavage on full display, whispering to Ryan and Micah in hushed tones, "Still no answer. Something is really wrong here."

"I agree."

"Yeah, obvi," Micah added, sassy and unhelpful.

"What do you guys think we should do?" she asked. "I've worked here a long time, but I've never had to deal with something like…this."

"How should we know?" Micah asked. "We're just a pair of teachers."

"I don't think we should leave. It's dangerous out there. I don't think anyone can get very far with this windstorm ripping its way through town." Ryan began, scratching the back of his head once again. "So, I think we wait here. It's safe here, safe enough anyway. We're all still alive, right?"

Micah shrugged, and Jade nodded, pausing to give Ryan a momentary once-over.

As the three formed a tentative plan to stay put, they looked out into the dimly lit room. The old man was chugging beer after beer at an impressive rate. The younger duo wiped their eyes, shedding stray tears, but generally holding their composure, and the red-haired woman paced back and forth with an indignant expression on her face.

"I think I might need just one more beer, Jade," Ryan said. "I don't know how many dead people I've seen today, but it's definitely too many."

Instead, Jade pulled a bottle of The Knot from under the counter and grabbed three shot glasses. "I think we need something a little stronger right now. Sound good, fellas?" While Jade's practiced facade came off as calm and collected, she was obviously far from it.

"I'd prefer a chocolate cake shot myself, but if

it's free, count me in. I like my drinks free," Micah said.

Jade poured a round, and they gave a quick 'salud' before clinking their glasses on the bar and tipping the sweet liquid down their throats, feeling its sting as it slid down to warm their bellies.

"One more?" Jade offered.

As she was pouring, an older woman, Ginger, stormed her way towards the front door, all feathered hair and outrage. "I'm done with this! I'm out of here!" she screeched before shoving herself between the furniture they'd piled up to block the door. In her outrage, she began pounding on the security door to get out.

"Stop that!" Jade yelled, too far to physically restrain the woman. "Do not pound on my door, Ginger!"

With the sturdy door locked and blockaded, Ginger wasn't making much progress, but with her temper flared, she kept at it, battering the door over and over with her manicured fists.

"Ginger, no. It's not safe," Jade pleaded, slowly making her way across the room. "I need you to stop. Go sit down and cool off. You need to remain inside for now."

"I'm not staying here cooped up. This is nonsense. No one tells me what to do. Do you hear me? This is America. I have rights. I'm free to do as I please, and I'm certainly not taking commands from a common bartender." She took a key from her pocket and jammed it into the slit between the door and its frame, attempting to use it as a lever.

"Ginger, seriously, stop. You're going to bust my door. And I will make you pay for it. Those doors aren't cheap."

"Well, you have no right to keep me, to keep any of us here. I'm allowed to leave whenever I damn well please. Stop oppressing me. I'm not a prisoner, and I refuse to let you keep me under lock and key. What are you going to do next? Chain me up? You young people think you can do anything you want, but you can't!" With that, Ginger returned to her task, managing to damage the seal, creating a tiny space for air to leak in.

A small draft spindled in through the crack in the doorway, cold and menacing. Though it wasn't visible to the naked eye, the wind carried with it the scent of oak trees and smog. As it slithered into the building, bit by tiny bit, it wrapped itself around the older woman's neck, spiraling around her petrified form like a coiling snake and lifting her from the ground.

"What's happening?" Ginger yelled, her voice quivering. "What's happening to me? Someone help! Get me down from here!"

The incident felt drawn out like it happened

over the course of several agonizing minutes. But, it took mere seconds, barely enough time for everyone's eyes to go wide at the horrific display. With Ginger entirely in its hold, the air crushed from her smoker's lungs, her last breath expelling outward in a strangled puff. The wind made a sound that could have been mistaken for a laugh, almost as if it enjoyed causing the awful woman pain.

For a second, Ginger was almost floating in front of everyone before the winds pulled her hard back toward the door and smashed her body against the metal frame, over and over, widening the gap ever so slightly until she hung limp in the air like an oversized rag doll, still and dead, blood trickling from the corner of her mouth, tears dripping from her still open eyes.

Ryan made a mad dash for the door and removed the key Ginger had wedged into the crack, covering the remaining hole with his hand. The wind nipped at his flesh, causing a sensation akin to burning. With the wind interrupted, Ginger's corpse fell to the floor with a heavy, wet thud. The crack of her neck, loud as she hit a table's edge on her way down, would have certainly killed her if she hadn't already been dead. Head bent at an unnatural angle, Ginger's corpse was horrific. Her open eyes looked out into the bar, glassy and no longer seeing and her skin was torn where her neck had broken, the tip of a white bone protruding from the small hole. Blood trickled from her orifices, streaming down her face, and dripping onto the floor.

"Hey, this kinda hurts. Can someone get some tape or something to seal up this hole? Please? Like now?" He wasn't issuing orders, but there was a tinge of urgency in his deep voice.

Jade sprang into action, digging into her junk drawer and finding a roll of duct tape, which she tossed at Micah, who ran it over to Ryan. Micah made quick work of taping up the hole and then taping over tape and taping tape over more tape, just in case.

"Doesn't that look spectacular?" he asked; his handiwork looked like a silvery starburst. "A masterpiece."

"Now might not be the time, Micah."

"What? Why? I didn't even plan it this way. The art just happened. Talent, that's what I call it," he replied.

"Someone just died…in a real freaky and confusing way…we can look at your artwork later. I'm sure it's very nice."

"Oh, yeah," he replied, looking over to see Ginger's mangled body, "gross." He nudged Ginger's corpse with the toe of his loafer. "Yup.

She's kaput."

Ryan eyed his tactless friend and calmly said, "Let's just go back to the bar for now. Sound good?"

Micah nodded at Ryan, and then the two walked back toward Jade, feeling the eyes of the remaining patrons following their path. A hush had befallen the room.

"What do we do now?" Micah asked, looking to Jade for guidance.

"I don't know. This day didn't come with a manual," she replied. She was good at doing the books, and she could make a mean Manhattan, but leading a small group of refugees after witnessing something utterly impossible wasn't her strength.

Seeming pragmatic, Jade re-pointed out that the building was strong and had held up for ages, that they'd be safe inside for now. There was food, drink, and activities, and they had toilets. The group had plenty of room to spread out and could even make passable sleeping surfaces out of pool tables or rows of chairs if needed. There were six of them left, and the matter of tending to Ginger's unfortunate corpse was the logical place to start.

"So, what do we do with her?" Micah asked, pointing dramatically and sneering at the dead woman halfway across the room. "She's gonna start to smell."

"I don't think that happens for a while, Micah," Ryan offered. He'd studied human biology. He knew, as long as they weren't in a sweltering heat, that Ginger wouldn't stink the place up for some time.

"Sure, but does anyone really want to look at that?" Micah asked.

"I don't think you're supposed to move a dead body. Isn't that right? Or is that just a TV thing?" Ryan said.

Jade shrugged.

Wiping tears from her eyes, a young woman in the corner pleaded, "Can we move her, please? I don't think I can look at her…it…that… anymore."

"I guess we can put her in one of the freezers?" Jade offered.

"Okay, then," Ryan started, "this is not the day I signed up for."

Jade and Ryan dragged Ginger to the back kitchen and dumped her into a half-empty chest freezer before exchanging worried glances and sealing her up.

"Poor Ginger," Ryan remarked upon his return.

"Ah, glorious, out of sight, out of mind," Micah said.

"What's wrong with you, man? She was a human who lost her life."

"Yeah, I get that," he replied, rolling his eyes,

"but she was gross, Ryan. Did you hear all of her freedom nonsense? I'm not wrong here. Plus, like, she was warned. We told her to stay inside. We told her to stop. She chose this."

Ryan chewed on his lip, and gave a resigned "Okay, then," in reply. He eyed the red mark on his hand. It looked like a hickey, and he was sure it would bruise, but other than that, he was unscathed.

No one else had moved, not yet, but soft sobs and sniffles echoed across the quiet room.

Chapter Five: Earlier on Day One

Ms. Presswick, Janice, made her way to the front of the building, feeling great about the work she'd just done. Those educators needed her help and her brilliant ideas, and she'd spent the morning enlightening their minds. They'd all be better educators after hearing what she had to say; they *always are*, she thought.

She pulled out the fresh $3,000 check they'd handed her in a sealed envelope and kissed it. "Another day's work is done."

Getting into her Tesla, the woman kicked back, content to let it autopilot her into town so she could deposit her check and do some shopping before heading to her comfortable lakeside home. It wasn't the mini-mansion she'd grown up in, and she only had one housekeeper, but it was still an impressive house, one people were jealous of, and she loved having that kind of status in her community.

Once in town, she decided she'd earned herself an ice cream treat. So, she waddled her way to the quaint town's little frozen treats shoppe and ordered a triple scoop cone. Greedily, she licked the piled-up ice cream as it melted down the cone, making her thick fingers sticky and sweet to taste. The wind outside seemed concerning, so she didn't want to risk losing her treat on her way back to the car. She slurped down the ice cream with murmurs of pleasure between licks.

The young man at the counter, slightly grossed out by her sexual affair with the ice cream cone, turned away. Instead of leaving the shop, she remained rooted to the spot, moaning in an all too sexual manner.

Janice frowned once she'd finished the towering cone, her sticky fingers the only remnant of what she'd devoured. One by one, she stuck those meaty fingers into her mouth, sucking the rest of the confection from her flesh, before leaving the room with a "harumph."

"Thanks, come back again," she heard the counter boy call as the door jingled shut behind her.

A sturdy woman, Janice swayed in the wind as

the storm forced her forward. She fought to keep her balance, planting each foot down, one step at a time, with a decisive thump. "My, my, my, it's getting nasty out here."

Second-guessing her trip to the bank, she turned back toward her car. She wondered how the Tesla would fare in the maddening wind. Fighting against the wind as her stubby arms flailed along at her side, her progress was slow.

"Well, this just doesn't make sense," she said. "It can't be blowing both ways, can it? I don't think wind works that way."

Janice made a mental note to research more about wind when she got home. Perhaps I can start giving talks to storm chasers. That might be a nice new stream of income. *Yes, I think I'll be a wind expert next. I'm so talented and intelligent.*

Absorbed in her thoughts, she didn't notice when the atmosphere thickened; no longer did it feel like slogging through mud. It had gotten much worse. She was almost immobile, moving mere inches instead of feet. "What's going on here?" she demanded, though there was no one nearby to respond. She turned her head, agonizingly slowly, back in the direction of the ice cream parlor, but it was too far now, and the spaghetti-armed boy inside didn't seem very useful anyway. She figured the poor little cretin would sooner rob her than help her.

Panicked, her heart thumping hard against her chest, Janice's fear was spiraling out of control. *Stop, Janice, breathe. You can't get worked up like this. You know that. Calm down.*

Once her rational brain had taken over, she attempted to fumble for her phone, deep in her tight pants pocket. It took forever for her to slide a hand that far down her body and to pry open an aperture big enough to accommodate her fleshy digits. Meanwhile, the wind was pressing in on her, driving her toward the brick wall of the bakery behind her.

I've got it now, yes! She closed her hand around the phone and began the drawn-out process of extracting it from her pocket and bringing it out into the open so she could make a call for help. *There we go. It'll be alright soon—no need to worry.*

She managed to hit the emergency call button, turning on the speaker afterward since the process of bringing the phone to her ear felt like it might take too long. It was difficult to hear the phone over the wind whipping past her face, but the call showed as connected, and she could make out the *ring, ring, ring* on the other end, but no one answered. Panic rising again, Janice sputtered to herself, "Who doesn't answer a nine-one-one call?

How lazy!"

The faint *ring, ring, ring* continued with no response until the phone dropped the call with a decisive beep. "What? What's going on here?" She squinted at the phone, seeing an X in the corner where her bars were moments before. "Dammit! The phone company is going to get a piece of my mind. I better get a discount!"

As Janice was lost in her confused efforts, the menacing wind wrapped itself around her spongy arms, whipping them back in a quick, ferocious snap, breaking each humerus in half; bone shards punctured through the flesh and stuck out, white and unnatural. Janice screamed out into the void, "Heeellllp meeeeeee!" as she turned to look at her useless arms hanging there by skin flaps at her sides.

Still, her footing held. Stepping forward, she attempted to break free from the wall, but the steadfast wind kept her rooted to the spot. A swirl of wind rose up in front of her, gathering leaves and stray twigs, a micro-tornado spinning its way down to the ground. Blood coursed down her flapping arms, quick and red, while the wind jangled her broken limbs about like a fleshy wind chime. She swore that if the wind had a face, it would have been laughing at her. Leaving the distinct impression of something cruel and cold, the wind pressed forward once again, enveloping Janice in its funneling embrace. No longer able to screech out her entitled drivel, Janice was gagging on the wind, trying to gulp it down like she had her ice cream, swallow after swallow, but she couldn't keep up, eventually succumbing to the pressure, her lungs suffocating as she struggled for air.

The wind funneled inside of her as she choked, gasping while her lungs collapsed inward, and it pulled on her body, pushing her remaining breath out while shoving wind and various litter particles down her expanding throat. Wide-eyed, Janice was helpless to stop it. She tried to move her arms, but they remained useless at her sides. There was no way for her to block the wind.

She wasn't even able to scream, to notify someone of her attacker, to call for help. Done with its plaything, the wind withdrew from her lungs, and she gasped, thinking she'd prevailed, that she would indeed make it out of this one, hurt but alive, that she'd be able to enlighten more rooms full of needy educators. *I'm a survivor. Survivors make good money. Look out, world, I'm coming, and I'm ready for my close-up.*

But the wind reeled back, collecting itself into a solid sheet, and it smacked her against the brick wall, her skull fracturing in the back from the sheer force of the blow. Chunks of hair and skull fragments were glued to the wall by thick globs of blood which dripped down from the circular splatter from when her head smashed. And, like it had never been there, the wind dissipated, back into the more significant gusts working their way through the town.

Slumped, Janice twitched a few minutes more before her body ceased functioning. However, her brain fired a bit longer than that. In those few minutes, her life was stifled out, and she lay useless and discarded, alone, pinned up against that wall, broken and unnatural, watching the wind do something, maybe?

Chapter Six

The six remaining patrons all sat quietly, sipping drinks and unceremoniously crunching on salty pretzels. The televisions no longer broadcast anything but silence and static, which made their world much smaller. The electricity still hummed along, showing no signs of fading, and they'd been able to take turns charging their various electronic devices, existing on previously downloaded content and a small stack of sci-fi novels Jade had socked away in her office for slower days on the job.

An older man named Ed had taken over the

taps, grumbling something incoherent now and again as he worked. He'd grown comfortable with the surroundings almost immediately and was already expertly pulling his own beers. "Look, no foam," he exclaimed, proud of his newly minted bartending skills.

Shrugging, Jade let him do as he pleased. He wasn't hurting anyone, and the bar had more than enough beer to go around for days, weeks, even. Certainly, FEMA was going to come around and reimburse everyone for the damage, or maybe the insurance would cover costs. While the storm outside couldn't be called a natural disaster, it was still a disaster. If not, Jade knew she'd figure it out and that it was a problem for another day.

Liza and Jorge sidled up next to Ryan and Micah.

"Hi, I'm Liza," she said, extending her hand first to Ryan and then Micah, "and this is my little brother, Jorge."

Shuffling uncomfortably by her side, the younger boy nudged her, "I'm six-three; stop introducing me as little."

"What do you want me to call you? You are my little brother."

"I'm your younger brother," he said, correcting her.

"Fine," she responded, decisive and

mischievous, "then, this is my baaabbbyyy brother, Jorge."

"Ugh, you're the worst," Jorge said, before turning away and politely asking the bartender for a Long Island iced tea.

Jade offered a salute and turned to fetch several bottles from the shelf behind the bar.

Ryan cleared his throat. "Well, I'm Ryan. It's…uh…nice to officially meet you."

Micah nodded, only minimally interested, and followed with a simple, "Micah."

"So…" Liza began, "What can you tell us about this whole situation?" She haphazardly pointed to the taped-up door.

"I don't think we know much more than the rest of you. We've seen a little more, but we don't know anything for sure," Ryan said.

"What did you see?" she asked, twirling her hair around a finger.

Not picking up on her subtle attempt at flirting, the science-minded Ryan continued, "It's windy. And at first, I just thought there was a storm coming, maybe one that would turn into a tornado. But that's not what this is. I guess I don't know what it is because I can't begin to explain what happened to that woman."

"She died, and we stuffed her in a freezer," Micah offered unhelpfully.

Ryan rolled his eyes. "Let's not get into that, alright?"

"Yeah, sure, continue with your boring story." Micah went back to sipping a drink and reading the license plates that were nailed across the room's border.

"Anyway, sorry about that."

"That's alright," Liza said, lightly brushing his hand. "Go on."

"So, I think we can definitely call it a derecho now. Do you know what that is?"

Liza shook her head.

"Well, basically, it's a giant angry windstorm spread out across a large area. I'm not a physical geography guy, so I don't know the nitty gritty, but that's the basic premise."

"Okay, so there's a derecho, is it?"

"That's my best guess." He shrugged. "I've never seen anything like this."

"But that doesn't really explain why you ran in here, terrified. You don't barricade a door just because of a windstorm, do you?"

"I mean, it's probably not a terrible idea," Micah said, interrupting once again. "You wouldn't go running out into a tornado, would you?"

"There is a little more to it than that," Ryan said.

Jade had closed in, watching the conversation between Ryan and Liza unfold and feeling annoyed at the girl's flirting.

The five of them sat huddled together while the increasingly drunk old man, Ed, wandered aimlessly about the room.

"Just tell us what's out there," Liza said, tucking one of her curly brown locks behind her ear.

Ryan scratched the back of his head again. "Okay, well, when we tried to leave the first time, we found the dead body of a woman we'd heard speak at the college earlier."

"A super milquetoast woman, good riddance to her," Micah said.

"Micah, stop it. Yeah, she sucked at her job, and we had to sit there and listen, but she was still a person."

"Ugh, you're no fun," he replied. "Stop trying to ruin my amusing quips."

Ryan turned away from Micah without responding. "Anyway...so, that's when we came back the first time and tried to call for help."

Jade nodded as she absently wiped the counter with a damp bleach-scented rag.

"Just the woman?" Jorge asked, suddenly more interested in the conversation.

"No cars. No animals. Just the dead woman,

the roaring wind, and the light from this bar."

"That's not exactly true," Micah said. "There were other people out there. They just weren't alive anymore."

Liza gasped. "Wait? What?"

"Yeah," Ryan started again, "so, that's the thing, there were other dead people."

"Dead how?" Jorge asked.

"They were pinned to a wall out there, chunks of broken glass embedded in their bodies. It's like a scene out of a medieval war or something. So, that's…uh…a little more troublesome."

"That's when we ran back here," Micah said.

"And that's all? No one else?" Liza asked.

"As far as we saw, that was all, but there's no way of knowing. There might be people out there, alive or dead."

"Else?" Liza asked, the word thick on her tongue. "What else is there?"

"I don't know, but can you explain what we saw today? I certainly can't," Ryan said, a sense of finality in his voice.

"Well, no," she replied, looking concerned. She glanced over at her brother, who, half-drunk from his Long Island iced tea, seemed only partially concerned as he scrolled absentmindedly through photos on his cell phone.

After a few more minutes, the little group

broke up, and the brother/sister duo returned to their corner, whispering to one another. Since the bar had power, people were able to play darts and pinball to waste the time. The old jukebox, lit up in the corner and with a small selection of vinyl records. They resumed a facsimile of normality and wasted the night on bar games, digital books, and dated music.

By 3 AM, still not able to reach anyone, they decided to attempt to sleep. The bar had two comfortable leather chairs in one corner, and the rest of the chairs were padded enough that pushing a few together in a row against the wall made for a comfortable facsimile of a bed. The siblings claimed the corner chairs, which left Micah and Ryan assembling makeshift beds.

"I want one of those comfy chairs tomorrow. If we're staying for a few nights, we better rotate," Micah demanded.

The older man opted to sleep on the pool table. Jade bid everyone goodnight, shut out the main lights, leaving only the neon signs to light the room, and went to her office to get some rest.

While she'd slept in the bar multiple times, it'd never been out of fear. Sometimes, it was convenient just to stay the night. Other times, she'd overconsumed and didn't feel comfortable driving home. Tonight sleep found her swiftly as she collapsed from the day's stress.

The rest of the group wasn't as lucky. They'd tossed and turned for at least a half hour before hearing the familiar zip of someone's fly followed by a soft, metered thwapping sound. Wide-eyed, Micah looked over to Ryan, who raised his hands in the air as if to signal, 'not me.' Micah mouthed a quick 'what the fuck' before pointing over toward the pool table where they could make out small shuffling motions.

No one said anything. They didn't have the energy, and it didn't seem worth it. So, minutes later, most of them drifted away to the sounds of the old man jerking off on the pool table, right there out in the open for anyone to see.

—

As morning crested the horizon, the bar patrons awoke, disgruntled and slightly disoriented. Jade came out of the back office, stretching but looking refreshed. "Good morning, everyone. Does anyone want something to eat?"

She was met with a chorus of grumpy and groggy yesses.

"Alright, the kitchen has plenty of food. Eggs and bacon coming up."

"What about some toast?" Micah asked.

"We do have bread. Does someone want to come back here and grill it up?" Jade asked.

"I can," Ryan offered, yawning. "I'm a buttered toast whiz."

In the kitchen, Jade joked with Ryan, and they laughed together while preparing what wound up being quite the feast.

As everyone sat at the bar, moaning over crisp bacon and scrambled eggs, Jade offered to call 911 again as soon as they were finished eating. Liza and, begrudgingly, Jorge offered to do the dishes as a thank you. The others followed suit, pitching in where needed.

Jade dialed 911, hoping that the storm had died down and people were available again, but she was met with an endless *ring, ring, ring*. Spirits waning, the group kept to themselves, reading Kindle books on their phones or playing mobile games. They made use of the pool table, even though its reputation had been besmirched.

The afternoon bled into evening. No one tried to enter the bar, and no one tried to exit. The phone on the other side of their 911 calls endlessly rang, never reaching a human, never reaching help. The group took turns trying to call other numbers, but it was much of the same, just ringing and voicemail messages. Cell service did not return.

"Alright, I guess we're calling it a night again," Jade declared after they'd finished cleaning up the dinner dishes and had a nightcap.

"Not much else to do, is there?" Micah asked, "But I want one of the comfy chairs tonight."

Liza, not wanting to cause her brother discomfort, offered to let Micah take hers for the night.

"Thank you," he said, sauntering by and plopping down on the comfy worn chair,

Feeling grimy and disheveled, everyone else made their way to a sleeping surface and turned in for the night. The bar was silent, save for the hum of the neon signs, a light buzzing in the background, and the sounds of Ed briefly wrestling his snake.

—

I am patient, especially where devastation is concerned. There are small living snakes to keep my cravings at bay, to save me from famine. These cowering humans pose a challenge, but I am endless and eternal and can wait until they slip up, until their stores run dry. They will provide a most satisfying meal, yes. Indeed.

Chapter Seven: Earlier on Day One

Ernest Goldberg, nearing the end of his shift, zipped his blue windbreaker tighter. The draft was picking up, and a cold breeze rustled through the trees, chilling him more than he'd anticipated.

Thankfully, he'd worn the jacket today. The short sleeves of his uniform wouldn't have shielded him from the biting wind even if he kept up his near-perpetual motion.

He worked the early shift. He'd leave the house around 3 AM so that he'd have enough time to stop for coffee on his way to work. By 4 AM, he was stuffing his personal possessions into a locker in the back of the post office and getting his truck loaded. On a good day, he could be done with the mail and headed home by the time kids were getting out of school. The long days, ones fraught with problematic customers or loose dogs, went much later. Still, even working a 10-12-hour shift was worth it for the paycheck and government pension plan. The job even kept him fit without the need for a gym membership or a Peloton bike.

"Morning, Mike," he called to the Postmaster as he finished loading up his truck for the day.

"It's getting windy out there, Ernie. Drive safe!"

"Great, you know how I love driving a giant metal box with no door in the wind." Ernest laughed, gritting his teeth a bit and hoping the weather would calm down sooner rather than later. He honestly didn't want to deal with hundreds of envelopes during a windstorm. It was his worst goddamn nightmare.

"Ha, yeah, I remember those days," Mike started. "These old bones wouldn't even make it down the block anymore. Thank goodness for front desk duty."

"I can't wait," Ernest replied. "Plus, the regulated weather in this bad boy is a dream come true."

"You'll get there, kid. Don't rush your youth. Enjoy it while you have it. Get out there and breathe in some fresh air. You'll feel better."

"I'll do that, but I'll still be dreaming of selling stamps in the temperate post office once I've done my turn delivering mail."

"It has its perks. But don't forget I also get to deal with my fair share of awful customers…and there's nowhere to run. I'm stuck behind this counter all day. You have the ability to run away. I, sadly, do not."

"That does sound terrible, but it beats melting in the hot hundred-degree sun and slogging through three feet of snow, I'm sure."

"That's fair. Have a good day." Mike waved, laughing at Ernest.

Whistling, Ernie checked to make sure his thermos was full before heading out for his shift. While the wind seemed a little heavy, especially so early in the day and with no storm clouds of note, he didn't think it'd impede his deliveries too much as long as it didn't get worse. *Fingers crossed the weather holds.*

The truck jostled a bit as he drove along, but the early part of the route was all city streets and 25 miles per hour speed limits, not exactly risky conditions. As the wind whipped in his face, Ernie flipped down his sunglasses and parked so he could hop out with his first deliveries.

"Hey, Ms. Jones." He waved while stuffing a handful of flyers and predatory loan offers into a mailbox.

"Good morning, Ernest. It's getting windy today. You stay safe out there."

"So it seems! Thanks, see you tomorrow." He waved again before hopping back into the truck with his empty canvas satchel.

Ernie took a swig of ashy coffee, noticing the wind had picked up a bit in the last hour or so. Little dust devils swirled around in the road, and the temperature felt cooler, too. Still, he felt like he could keep a decent pace and get home before having to deal with the school buses.

The second leg of his route took him through the downtown area, and while he did have deliveries, the biggest responsibility he had was emptying the blue mailboxes littering the central area of town. It was time-consuming and required some back and forth. He was less excited about fighting against the wind while he ran to and from the mailboxes with his hands and bag full of heavy letters and packages. He liked using the mail bins for this particular job, but with no covers, he was afraid mail would flit away on the wind. *Well, today is going swimmingly.* He sighed, readying himself for burning thighs and a little extra sweat.

The wind tickled his neck as he walked down the street. Shop doors were closed, and people were sparse. The town was usually bustling in the afternoon, but the wind had probably kept them at home. He could understand that even he held fast to the USPS motto. In some ways, he preferred the quieter streets. Navigating through crowds made him a little anxious. Solitude felt natural, which made him well-suited to his work. He was on his own most of the day, and his interactions with others were brief. *Maybe I would hate desk duty. Mike may have been right.* His delivery work kept him busy, and he could listen to several audiobooks a week, a perk he didn't take for granted.

Whistling as he fought against the wind, steps becoming slightly more difficult, despite well-condition leg muscles, Ernest grew annoyed. *This kinda sucks. Where is this stupid wind even coming from? There isn't a damn cloud in the sky.*

Even though it had taken him an hour longer than usual, he was finally parked by his last blue mailbox, the one near the cheese shop. The wind felt almost unnatural at this point, and it lapped at his neck and nipples in a tingling way that wasn't all that unpleasant. *Great, I'm getting horny now. What's even going on? Maybe I need a vacation or a girlfriend or both.*

The wind continued to caress the mailman in slightly inappropriate ways.

Ernie continued, an empty bin in hand, toward the mailbox, wanting to get things over with so he could head to the hospital with his final round of mail. He'd grabbed a brick off a trash pile; he had been using it to hold the mail down. The extra weight was annoying, but it had saved him some of the back and forth. The storm was getting to be too much for him, and the truck felt like it was going to blow off the road the last time he moved it, but the mail needed to be delivered. So, he soldiered on. The USPS trusted him to stay on track and to get mail in boxes, a feat he took seriously, even in dangerous situations. But he was trying to hurry things along as best he could.

Ernie squatted in front of the mailbox, setting the bin to his left but forgetting to weigh it down. The wind scooped it up within seconds, and he was caught between chasing it and just letting it fly away. No one really cared about one bin, and he still had his bag and hands with which to transport the mail. Sighing, he unlocked the door at the bottom of the box and peered in. It wasn't terribly full. So, he decided the bin was unnecessary and hoped someone would find and return it tomorrow. He'd leave the brick below the box, too, not needing to carry it back with him anymore.

As his head was inside the box, he heard the shattering of glass nearby, followed by a chorus of angry yelling and terrified screams. *What's going on?* Quickly, he removed his head, turning slowly toward the sound. His eyes went wide as he attempted to decode what he was seeing: people thrashing and almost flying around the cheese shop behind him. *What the hell?*

—

Mary Haskins, a 16-year-old sociopath, stood near an alleyway dumpster. She'd been watching idiots run around in the wind for hours. While amusing, she'd grown bored even after finding a stupid old frump with broken arms down the block. She poked the lady with a stick for a while, but that was only fun for a few minutes. She'd been hoping the old gal had some life left in her. That, she decided, would have been delightful to watch. Mary wasn't terribly interested in already dead bodies, but they were adjacent to her dark desires. So, she didn't consider the experience a total loss.

Not understanding the frantic nature of the

richies in town, it didn't seem all that windy to her as she skipped freely down the street, the wind caressing her young face in an almost maternal gesture. Everyone else acted like this was a wind tunnel or that they were treading up invisible hills, which she found hilarious if not mildly concerning. *Have all these privileged bastards lost their minds? Did I stumble into a weird flash mob of slow-motion mimes? These people look ridiculous.* While Mary felt the wind in her hair, slapping her ponytail hard against her neck, she was able to waltz freely. She skipped past people as they forced tiny steps, one foot in front of the other.

However, she didn't mind the frantic people; they were almost preferable. The idiots dropped things or, in the case of the dead woman, had purses to rob. It was a productive and profitable day for Mary. She'd made off with rings, a giant bag of Taco Bell, $200 cash, and a check for a couple thousand written out to cash—all in all, not a bad day.

But, busy looting and pillaging, she'd yet to see anything like the carnage going on across the street. A high-pitched scream, carried by the wind, caught Mary's attention. Peeling the paper from another taco, she bit down with a decisive crunch and chewed the cold, salty concoction as several people violently died in front of her eyes. Finishing her taco, she dug in the bag for more food and pulled out a crunch wrap. "Sweet, I love these." She watched, eyes alight with desire, while she masticated her stolen fast food. The deaths across the street were a massive blood-filled gore fest, better than any b-horror movie she'd ever seen; it was probably the best thing she'd ever witnessed. She particularly enjoyed the excessive amount of viscera. "Cool," she said, the word slipping from her lips with bits of spittle and tortilla chunks.

Wanting to get a closer look, she finished her crunch wrap, crumpled the paper, and tossed it to the ground before stashing her things in a nearby dumpster and waltzing across the street. Mesmerized by the arterial spray, she'd failed to notice the young mailman kneeling near an open mailbox. *I bet there are treasures in there. I never get packages. I think I'll have some today.*

Then she saw him. She picked up a terracotta pot off the sidewalk on her way over and decided to cause a little pain herself. She felt a windy pat on the back during her approach. The mailman looked horrified or in shock, maybe both. She leaned over, tapping him on the shoulder. "Hey there, buddy," she chided gleefully before bringing the pot down onto his head.

He choked out a small squeak as he fell, and she smashed him again to make sure he was at least unconscious. "This is fun!" she squealed. No one paid her any attention while she robbed the big blue box right downtown.

The mailman stilled, and she dug through the open mailbox, looking for packages. She made a small stack at her side, and while the wind seemed to be picking things up around her, it never touched her treasures. She patted her unconscious friend down but found nothing of note. *Damn. Stupid mail guy.*

A small groan escaped the mouth of the man she'd hit, and Mary smiled while picking up a broken shard of terra cotta. "I've never killed anyone before," she said, though the man wasn't awake enough to understand or respond. "You, sir, care to be my first?"

She looked around, noticing how truly empty the streets were. She and the mailman were the only living creatures in sight. "And, there's no one here to stop me, no witnesses to rat me out," she said, breathing her cheesy taco breath into his ear. "How perfect. Thank you. I've always wanted to do this."

With that, she drove the flowerpot shard into his neck. The flesh was harder to puncture than she'd anticipated. It took both of her tiny hands and a bit of weight to pop her weapon through the surface. Dragging the piece across his neck, she was able to create a gash wide enough for blood to spill from. "Awesome," she said, enchanted by the hot flow spurting out onto the sidewalk and splashing some of the white envelopes inside of the mailbox. "I wonder how long it'll take you to die."

She grabbed the man's wrist, feeling for a pulse, and picked up the intense throbbing of his life force. "Still alive, then, boo." Sitting there, his hand in her lap, she counted the seconds. At the three-minute mark, she was a little impressed with the guy and a little bored of waiting. His pulse slowed in that final minute until she felt nothing at all. "Four minutes. That's much longer than I thought it'd take. Good for you, pal. You're a champ."

She gingerly placed the man's hand back on the sidewalk and stood to admire her handiwork. Kicking him for good measure, just to make sure he'd actually died, Mary felt powerful—no movement, just like the lady from before. The wind smacked at her back twice, more demanding than before, in a gesture that felt like an *atta girl* before she made her way back across the street, arms full of yellow and white paper packages. She retrieved the rest of her goodies from the dumpster, shoving the boxes into her worn backpack, and decided to call it a night. She was getting tired anyway.

Merrily, she skipped home, barely noticing the wind as she went, respecting the devastation it had wrought throughout the day. It felt as if the wind was her friend. She liked that thought.

Chapter Eight

"Hey, Ryan, can I talk to you for a minute?" Jade asked. "Alone."

Curious, Ryan nodded and followed her into the back room. They'd been cooped up in the bar for almost four days, and people were stinky and on edge. He thought Jade might want to discuss some kind of exit strategy.

While the bar was safe and they still had plenty of provisions, electricity and water included, no one wanted to spend the rest of their life cooped up in a bar with people they barely knew, especially if one of those people was a masturbating older man. They'd run out of food at some point, too, and Ryan hoped that point hadn't come just yet. They weren't ready or equipped to go out into the madness, and there'd been no sign of life other than their own.

Jade closed and locked the door behind them.

"Is everything okay?"

Without saying a word, Jade sashayed across the room, removing her AC/DC t-shirt in the process. She unhooked her black bra, letting her breasts bounce free. Ryan stared at her, eyes wide, not expecting this turn of events. He watched as she jiggled, distracted by her naked mounds of flesh, and noticed a beauty mark near her right nipple.

"Uh…what's…" he began.

"Shhhh…" she said, placing a finger against his lips. "Not now."

She pushed him against the wall, crushing his lips with her own. She tasted of salt and cinnamon whiskey. Stiff at first, Ryan loosened up as the woman tangled her fingers in his hair and began to pull lightly. A struggled moan escaped his lips as her tongue made its way into his mouth, caressing his in expert strokes while she rubbed her body against him. Her need filled the room as her kisses grew more urgent and insistent.

He pulled back for a moment to look at her. "This is, um, unexpected?"

"How thick are you?" she asked, laughing at her joke. "I've been sending you signals for days, and I need to get rid of some of this pent-up energy. Sound good?"

"You have? I, uh, guess I missed those?"

"Did you miss Liza's too?" she asked, playfully but perhaps also a little jealous.

"What? What are you talking about?" he sputtered.

"You really are that dense, huh? Well, how's this for direct?" she asked, reaching down to unbutton her jeans and pushing them to the floor.

Ryan was already straining against his zipper,

but seeing her like that, naked and wanting him, made him harder, something he hadn't thought possible. Thankful he didn't need to make that first move, one that he probably never would have made, Ryan was ready and willing to do whatever Jade wanted.

Jade pushed him down onto the couch, unzipping his pants and freeing his stiff cock. It sprang upward, bouncing as she held it down and let it go over and over for her amusement. *Boink.*

Stepping back, she pushed her silly panties to the floor and stood there in just her fuzzy socks, then asked, "Are you ready?"

Unable to comprehend this situation, he simply nodded: 'Yes.'

"Good," she said as she straddled him, letting him slip inside of her excited pussy. "Mmmmhhmmm, that's what I need."

She rode him for several minutes before deciding they needed to change positions. Standing up and letting him withdraw from inside of her, she opened the back door into the kitchen and pushed him up against one of the chest freezers. "How strong are your legs?" she asked. "Can you do it standing up?"

Again, he nodded.

"That's what I like to hear."

Ryan grabbed her from behind as she hopped

up and wrapped her legs around his back, letting him enter her once more. Sweat dripping between her breasts, she moaned as he tipped her over the edge, the release she'd been seeking, before letting himself finish inside of her. She felt satiated and warm as she climbed down off him.

A look of horror crossed Ryan's face. Jade frowned.

"What's wrong? Was that bad?" she asked.

"Ahhhh, no, that was…that was great, but…" he trailed off, eyes dropping to the chest freezer they'd just fucked against. "I think we just had sex on top of Ginger."

Jade let loose a torrent of wild laughter, loud and free. "Oh my god, we did."

"Is that bad?" Ryan asked. "I think that's bad."

"Well, let's let it be our little secret," she replied.

"I don't think any of what just happened will be a secret. This place isn't exactly bustling and noisy."

As the two exited the office after having redressed but still stinking of sex, no one would meet their eyes. Ryan blushed, having had his sexual encounter pretty much broadcast to the whole bar. Liza, arms crossed and huffy, sat in the corner next to Micah, who was in a remarkably similar fashion. Jorge looked up, accidentally making eye contact with Ryan, which he followed with a sheepish thumbs up. Ed, still not speaking, looked over at Jade and unconsciously licked his chapped lips.

—

Days passed. By this time, most of them had lost count of how many. One week, maybe two, and yet no one had come to check on them. No other patrons had wandered by or knocked, attempting to get into the bar. And the phone on the other end of the 911 calls would simply *ring, ring, ring* without answer. No FEMA, no nothing.

Since the wind still raged on outside of the bar, Ryan suspected everyone was busy and that they'd probably elected to clear out things like the hospitals and schools first. Their little bar was a low priority, but as long as the light remained, he had hope that someone would come knocking sooner or later.

For now, Ryan and Jade would steal away into darkened corners or bathroom stalls to fuck when the itch reached its breaking point, but they learned to be quieter about it. Everyone still knew, but they weren't rubbing it in their faces. Their relationship blossomed into something safe and familiar, a sexy comfort during a trying time. He didn't know what would happen once they left the bar, but he was going to make the best of their time together.

"I fucking hate it here," Micah proclaimed, irritable and despondent. "I want to go home. My creativity is stifled in this cold space. Do you know what that does to an artist? This industrial building is a thief of joy."

"We all want to go home, man; all of us are stuck. As much as I love washing my clothes in a bar bathroom, I'd really like to change," Ryan replied.

"You seem to be doing just fine," Micah spat, pettily, "just fine."

"Okay, dude. I'm just trying to be kind. You don't have to jump down my throat." Ryan scoffed, not understanding why Micah had been so snippy the last several days. "This isn't ideal for any of us, but we're safe and warm and fed. That's gotta count for something."

"Uh huh," Micah replied noncommittally.

—

The days went on, in and out, until everyone was frayed and worn. While their food stocks were still solid, a captive life in the bar didn't seem sustainable to any of them anymore. They were cramped and uncomfortable, feeling trapped like rats and in need of a bit of freedom. Micah was the first to reach the breaking point, but they'd all eventually followed suit.

Liza and Jorge paced the bar for one hour every

afternoon in an attempt to get some exercise. But, as the days wore on, they began to lose motivation. They attempted things like push-up and sit-up challenges, using their innate sibling rivalry to fuel the fire as long as possible. But that, too, wore thin after a while. Jorge used a permanent marker to draw a hopscotch grid on the floor, which amused the siblings for a day or so.

"You know what I wish we had?" he asked his sister.

"No, what?"

"A kickball." He laughed at the thought.

"What would you do with a kickball in here? Break everything?"

A smile spread across Jorge's face. "No," he began, "we could play four square!"

Liza laughed. "What are we, eight? Haha. Foursquare."

"Hey, that game is fun, and you can't deny it."

"I haven't played in like a decade," she replied, brightening at the prospect of an adult game.

Everyone else side-eyed the brother-sister duo, not understanding their amusement and not interested in trying to. Still, at night, the group would play darts or pool, keeping track of wins in one of Jade's server ticket books. They attempted to be inventive but were hamstrung by their location and supplies.

Eyeing up the eight ball, Micah brought up going home again. "How long are we going to stay here? I've got a life to live."

"We all do, Micah," Jade replied. "We've been over this, and we've all agreed to stay until help arrives. It's just a matter of time. The world didn't end out there."

"You don't know that. Maybe it did," he spat in return, his hatred for the woman visibly roiling just under the surface.

"Well, if it did, what's there to go back to then?" she countered.

Micah was salty and grew more reclusive as time passed. He watched Jade and Ryan with the eyes of a scorned would be lover, seething at their budding romance from a far corner of the bar. Ryan, oblivious to Micah and his desires, only saw a grown man sulking rather dramatically.

Jade dealt with Micah as best she could, using kid gloves when necessary and being blunt where appropriate. It was obvious what he was going through and it wasn't her place to interrupt his emotional process. Still, she'd found companionship with Ryan in the unlikeliest of places, and it wasn't something she was going to let go of either. It kept her sane most days.

The group discussed leaving several times, but no one had tried since Ginger's unfortunate death.

It didn't seem wise. If there'd been any inkling of hope, they'd have taken the shot, but there was nothing. Radio static, endlessly ringing phones, and the ever-present whipping of wind. The door rattled now and again, but nothing had penetrated their fortress. The Ginger incident faded as the days passed by, their belief still suspended. No one could rationalize what they'd witnessed, and at some point, they'd all stopped trying.

As they sat in silence, sipping vodka-heavy screwdrivers, finally, in a lucid moment, Ed spoke. "We can't stay here forever, right?" His voice was hoarse and gruff. He'd grumbled and grunted his way through the past several weeks. So, his interjection was somewhat monumental as far as their makeshift society went.

They looked around the room, knowing that leaving was inevitable, and Jade offered a kind and generous, "No, but we can stay until my cupboards are empty. It'll last a while longer. This place was stocked full when everything went down, and with so few of us, it's not time to worry just yet."

"We appreciate the hospitality, but what about our families? Jobs? The world?" Ed pleaded.

Micah sneered and said, "I don't know, Grandpa, no one has come looking for us. Maybe they don't care anymore or maybe they're gone. Do you really think anyone else is alive out there?

Wouldn't the emergency line be working by now?" In his short tirade, the spark of Micah's flair and attitude returned. The man loved to fight.

"You know my name, Micah; stop calling me grandpa. I know you like to be rude, but this is important. We need to really consider our options," Ed began, reasonably logical for a man who'd been in a half-drunken stupor for days. "And, yes, I have to believe they're alive. I do. Maybe they're holed up like we are. We have no means of communication. Anything could be happening out there. I have a daughter and a granddaughter. I can't believe they're just gone. I can't."

"Ugh," Micah began, "you do remember that the fucking wind killed a woman right before our eyes, right? I hate it here. Let's be clear. I know I've grumbled about leaving, but I was just being a dick. That incessant wind is still clawing at this old building, and I don't want to open that door. I like being alive."

Placing a wrinkled hand on his hip, Ed continued, "Yes, but we can't stay here forever. The resources are finite. We'll eventually die here of starvation. I've seen what that does to a person. It's a slow and agonizing death. I wouldn't want that for any one of you. So, we can stay here and wait for death, or we can take our chances outside."

Micah considered the man before replying.

"Look, I hate being trapped, probably more than all of you combined. But I hate the idea of dying more. So, I, for one, am content to stay for now. We've got everything we need to survive. We don't have to make big choices today." Micah looked out to the rest of the group, who nodded their heads one by one. "See, everyone else agrees."

"Ed," Liza began, "why don't we wait until we're a little closer to the point of no return? We're safe here, right? Happy enough? If we get through to emergency services, great. If we don't, well, we can cross that bridge when we need to."

"Fine," he replied, returning to his relative silence and slogging over to the bar to pull himself another beer.

After that, things settled into a calm routine again. The other patrons were non-confrontational and content to ride out the storm, and they did. Micah, having been sparked back to life by the old man, had made it his personal project to create an art installation in the bathroom. It was an oddly beautiful found object piece, mainly made from discarded cans and bottle caps.

As Micah was in the middle of hauling an armful of discarded bottle caps to the bathroom, he noticed Jade tugging at the belt loops of Ryan's jeans. She motioned for Ryan to follow her into the back office, and Micah frowned, his face reddening with anger. He scoffed at their orchestrated dance, took several deep breaths, and continued his trek to the bathroom to add to his instillation piece.

Once in the back office, Ryan made quick work of unzipping his fly.

"Wait," Jade cautioned, "we're not back here for that. Not yet, anyway."

He paused, sheepish with a fast-fading grin on his eager face. "Oh, ah, sorry. I just kinda assumed...my bad."

"No, it's fine. It's best if everyone thinks we're in here naked anyway," she said, leaning in, her voice a whispered hush.

"Okay, why?"

"We're running low," Jade wrung her hands, concern crossing her brow, "on food, Ry. We're running low on food."

"Ah, well, that is a problem." He pondered for a moment. "How low are we?"

"I don't know. It's not super dire yet, but we have a week, maybe two, if we ration things out. I think there's probably a little more food in the freezer with Ginger, but I've been avoiding it because that feels a little gross. If we get in there and move it all out, and if we're cool eating it, there might be another week or two. But, still, that's yucky."

"I mean...it is, a little. But the food is

packaged. I'm sure it's fine to eat. Beggars can't be choosers, yeah?"

"We'll go through what's left first, but that's that. With the food in the other freezer, I think we have like a month. Tops. The booze will last longer. We have tons, but that's not going to keep anyone alive. Hell, it'll probably kill us faster. And we've got running water. But that's not going to help us very long either."

"Do you think someone could leave and go scavenge one of the nearby businesses for food?" Ryan offered.

"I don't know. I guess we won't know unless we try to open the door again. But this stuff isn't going to be finite. We need a longer-term solution. This bar wasn't meant to house half a dozen people, obviously."

"No, no, you're right," he agreed, "We can't just grow old as a weird group of shut ins. This isn't *Gilligan's Island*."

She took his hand and looked at him thoughtfully. "Would that be so bad? We've got a good thing going here, you and me."

"This is a horrible suggestion, but just to make things last a little longer, have you thought about…"

"Eating Ginger?" she finished. "Yes, I've thought about it. I don't know if I could do that,

PLAYING HOOKY

even if it means dying."

"I don't either," Ryan replied, though if pressed, anything was possible. "I don't either. But, since we're in here, you wanna get naked?"

Jade laughed, nodding yes, ready to lose herself in the moment and forget the bad for just a little while.

Chapter Nine: Earlier on Day One

The Cheese House, an eclectic shop in the heart of town, was bustling, an afternoon rush. The shop itself was one of the rare places frequented by both locals and tourists. It offered the largest selection of cheeses and smoked meats in the county and was run by really decent folks, kind and jovial. Of course, they couldn't keep up with big box stores, but they were fair and treated customers well.

The desire for cheese, meats, and various candies had shoppers facing the elements. A good Munster was worth braving the harsh winds.

"Do you have Munchee yet? No one has Munchee anymore! It's my favorite cheese," Antwoine said, almost pleading with the cheesemonger behind the counter.

"Sorry, Antwoine, it's hard to find. We don't have any today."

"Damn. Well, are there any other soft, sweet,

white cheeses?" he asked.

"Um, I can get you sweet and white but not soft, or soft and sweet but not white, not all three; which one strikes your fancy?"

"I don't know, surprise me," he offered, hoping he'd get something palatable even if it wasn't Munchee.

"Do you like fruit cheeses? We have a blueberry white cheddar and a cranberry white cheddar."

"Blueberry, maybe. Let's go with that," Antwoine replied, thinking cranberry might be too sour.

"Okay, I'll get you a brick. You want slices or cubes?"

"Let's do slices, please."

"Be right back," he replied before heading toward the cheese case.

Four others were wandering about, carrying small metal baskets and tossing shelved products in as they perused the stock.

"It sure is windy today," offered a white-haired older woman in a pink cardigan. "I should have worn my coat. I hope I don't catch a chill. My son will never let me hear the end of it if I get sick again. He told me to wear my coat, but I just didn't want to. It's too heavy and too scratchy."

A man to her left nodded. "Yeah, it's a nasty

wind, but I'm sure you'll be fine."

The shop lights flickered as a high-pitched whistling sound filled the room. The older woman gasped, and the cheesemonger said, "Shit," having cut his finger on the slicer when the lights went out.

Everyone in the store turned toward the window, curious about the noise and too nosy not to investigate. The sound grew louder and shriller, but nothing was visible beyond the window except a mailman emptying a mailbox and trees swaying heavily in the wind. As the sound intensified, the window itself began to vibrate.

"Um…" one of the patrons uttered, concerned, "what's that noise? Is this place shaking?"

"I don't think it's the shop," the cheesemonger called. "It's just the window."

Stretching beyond its limits due to the longevity and frequency of the sound filling the room, the window exploded inward in a shower of broken, jagged glass. Patrons with quick reflexes were able to get their arms up in front of their faces or turn and duck as the glass crunched and cracked its way into the store. Hundreds of shards embedded themselves into those arms and backs causing intense pain and heavy bleeding. Mostly, the patrons were intact with bloody though superficial injuries.

The older woman, slower than some of the

others, hadn't reacted. A large, jagged piece of glass had embedded itself in her right eye, splattering the ball into a useless lump of goo and reaching further into her ocular cavity before stopping, firmly implanted in her brain. Her mouth opened, but all that came out was a strangled poof sound. No scream. No struggle. She fell to the ground quickly, breaking a few small bones when she landed. Her motor functions impeded, she flailed momentarily in an attempt to remove the shard from her body. The woman's heart seized, a hand jerking to her chest as her body stiffened mid-convulsion; she died there on the ground. Even if they'd been able to call emergency services, she wouldn't have made it.

The cheesemonger, too, hadn't been as lucky. Inspecting the cut on his finger had distracted him, and when the window had exploded, he'd looked up, getting a face and neck full of glass. His deep voice rose when the screams escaped his body. Unlike the woman, he was able to pull glass from his face, slicing his other fingers in the process. Unfortunately for the man, one of the shards was firmly lodged in a major artery. He plucked glass from his pin cushion of a face and neck which loosened that particular chunk, blood freely flowed from the wound. He clapped a hand over the sizable hole to staunch the bleeding, but it wasn't enough to slow or stop the flow. As blood poured from the wound, he grew weak, slumping down against the counter. It took several minutes for him to lose enough blood to cause a death, and he spent those moments scared and crying in the corner.

In the havoc, the remaining shoppers failed to notice the wind filling the room, swirling around them, a new barrier to keep them in the shop.

"There'ssssssssss noooooo essscappppppeeeee." The blowing wind, swirling faster and faster, took on a sound that almost seemed like speaking. "Noooooo essscaappeeee."

Each living person was scooped up by invisible wind hands and squeezed uncomfortably, but not oppressively, as they were flung into the air. They kicked and flailed, attempting to break the wind's embrace, but none of them found a way out. Jostled about the room like dice shaking around inside an enclosed fist, the injured patrons screamed and cried out for mercy.

"Help us," a woman managed. "Someone help us."

Of course, there was no one there to help. The wind began to chuck its prisoners about the room one by one. The first woman landed on the counter, the receipt spindle having punctured the back of her neck through to her mouth; affixed to the counter and unable to move, she died there as her blood stained the day's tickets and dripped into the register's crevices on the lower shelf.

A larger man was thrashed about but eventually fell, backside down, across one of the store's metal shelving units. The fall alone didn't kill him, but the intense pressure pushed the glass already embedded in his back deeper into his spinal cord and kidneys. His end, a blessing that saved him from years of pain and misery, was filled with minutes of endless screams. His voice, growing hoarse, held out until his heart, too, ceased beating.

Metal posts jutting forward from the wall, the ones holding various bags of retro candies, were the final end for a woman named June Jenkins. When she was smashed into the wall, those shelving hooks served as de facto spikes, impaling her. She bled freely from dozens of open wounds, head lolling side to side as life left her body.

Antwoine was the last to die. The initial blast only damaged his right arm, ripping shallow gashes into his ashy skin. When dropped, his head hit the edge of the cheese counter, smacking hard, and a starburst filled his vision. His neck whipped backward, breaking a few vertebrae in the process. Bouncing from the counter and hitting the floor, his brain began to swell; he finally landed with his head peering behind the counter itself, which was the view he had when his consciousness returned.

From his vantage point, he spied a large box labeled *Munchee Cheese*, and he swore, "Those fuckers." Slowly, he crawled behind the counter and toward the box, keeping low and favoring his good arm. Without something to relieve the pressure in his head, he would die, but Antwoine didn't know any of this. Fingers outstretched, he touched the box, slowly pulling it toward him. Reaching in, he felt a sizeable pliant block of cheese, which made him forget the pain for a moment. Able to roll onto his back, clutching the cheese to his chest, Antwoine bit through the plastic wrap. The smell released directly into his nostrils. He peeled back the paper and greedily chomped down on the large brick, the cloying taste of soft cheese filling his mouth. As he swallowed, a chunk lodged in his throat, and before his brain injury could claim his life, he died, choking on Munchee cheese.

Chapter Ten

After a meager breakfast of breaded mushrooms and shriveling carrots, the group sat, somber, knowing something needed to change, and soon. Even the tubs of bar mix were mostly emptied, leaving a few peanuts and pretzels for the group to devour.

It was Ed who began the conversation for the final time. He looked at the sad people he'd barricaded himself in with all those weeks ago, having given them time to hope for a rescue. But none had come, and although no one said it out loud, he was sure they were running out of food. "I think you all know it's time to open the doors."

"We can still hear the wind out there," Ryan pleaded. "That thing, storm, monster, whatever it is, it's still out there. Do you really want to run right into it? That's certain death."

Ed considered Ryan's thoughts. "Unless it isn't. Staying in here is certain death. Eventually, we run out of food and drink, and starving to death is long and terrible. Even if that wind is out there, I'd prefer the quick death myself."

"That's really morbid, Ed," Micah responded. "Like, we all get that death is eventually coming, but we don't need to think about it right now. Maybe we will think about it next week, next month, or next year."

"You can't possibly think we can stay in here that long? It's clear our dear host is running low on food."

Jade avoided eye contact with Ed, which was confirmation enough of what he'd said.

"What if we don't want to leave?" Liza asked. "Jorge and I talked about it, and we're not comfortable going out there yet."

Ed grew exasperated, bending down with his head drooping between his legs. He took a few moments to breathe and collect himself before speaking. "I know, and I know you're all scared. But, if we stay, we're going to die. That's a certainty. Without food, you die. Out there, who knows? Maybe we have a chance? Maybe everything is fine?"

"Maybe, Ed, maybe," Micah replied, his sarcasm toned down, but only slightly.

Taking a leadership role was something Ryan had unwittingly stepped into. "I think there are a lot of complicated emotions running around here. But there is a third option. If you want to leave, you can. If you prefer to stay, you can. I think, as long as we do it quickly enough, we can get people outside without too much danger to the rest of us. Maybe?"

He didn't know, not really. The last time they'd opened the door, travesty had hit almost immediately. He hoped time had made it safer to open the door, but that was only conjecture. There was no way to know if what they'd been hearing was just regular wind or if it was something unspeakably worse.

"I don't think it's wise to stay in here much longer," Ed stated firmly. "But there isn't much else I can say."

"Liza and I want to stay, for now," Jorge said, taking the lead for once. "We don't want to go out into that thing."

Ed sighed. "Fine. Is anyone coming with me, then?"

Jade looked to Ryan, who looked to Micah. None of them were ready to step out into the unknown, even facing the harsh reality of starvation.

"I don't think so, Ed," Ryan said, speaking for the group.

"We do have food," Jade said, "and it won't last forever, but we've got a few weeks left before we'll be forced to go outside."

"I'm still leaving," Ed said, a strong sense of finality in his voice.

They moved their makeshift barricade away from the door, looking at the tape star Micah created to seal the hole Ginger had made. Thinking back to the incident filled everyone with anxiety and fear.

"Are you sure you want to do this?" Jade asked, partially worried for him and partially because she was worried for the rest of them.

"Let the masturbater go, Jade. Ta-ta." Micah laughed. "Just kidding, old man, be well. We hope you don't die."

Ryan cast a useless side-eye in Micah's

direction before sighing and shaking his head. Micah had been full of attitude since the beginning of the ordeal, and not the fun kind as it had been before the event, an impossible grating type.

"I can't stay here day in and day out, not knowing if my family is out there somewhere. If I can see my sweet granddaughter's smile just one more time, it'll be worth the risk. I'm ready to leave."

Stepping up, Ryan began ripping the duct tape from the wall, bracing himself for the worst.

"Wait," Ed said. "Why don't you let me do that? I'm the one leaving, after all."

Ryan stepped back, checking his pocket to make sure the roll of tape was nearby. He tipped his head at Ed.

As Ed ripped the final strip of tape from the door, and the wild wind howled past, he took a deep breath, unlocked the door, and opened it just a crack. Nothing violent slipped in, already an improvement from the last time they'd opened things up.

"If I find help, I'll come back. I promise," Ed said before blinking at the bright light and stepping out onto the sidewalk. He watched as Ryan stepped in to close and lock the door, an inkling of regret settling in.

Ed slowly made his way down the block. The

wind was terrible but nothing like what the two professors had described. The stench, though, was something altogether wretched. Rot, stinking in the hot sun. Ed didn't know what a dead body smelled like, but his brain immediately identified the scent as death, lots of it. It was enough to make him question what he'd been so confident of just moments before. He thought about going back, pounding on the door, and asking to be let in again, but he didn't want just to give up.

Ed peered out across the street and saw them there, the bloated corpses of folks splayed out against the building. They were, more or less, as the boys had described; hung up there along the wall in a disgusting display of violence. Long dead and rotting in the sunlight, they just hung there as warning, screaming at him to claw his way back into the bar.

"Why is no one out here? Why hasn't anyone cleaned this up?" he asked.

The wind momentarily stopped.

Ed attempted to break into a run, which wound up more of a quickened shuffle; he couldn't run much at his age, not with his aching hip. Rounding the corner, he stumbled over the corpse of a rotund middle-aged white woman who'd died in what looked like a painful and horrendous way.

"Jesus, what's going on out here?"

Sensing urgency, Ed made his way down the road past the ice cream shop. Swearing he sensed movement inside, but thinking it was impossible with all of the corpses just littered about the street, he carried on. His car was in the parking structure on the other side of the block, and he was nearly there.

He could see the concrete raised lot, full of cars but with no people in sight. The closer he got to his car, the more the wind picked up. Slowly at first but growing angrier and more oppressive with each step taken.

Shit, he thought, worry increasing with the intensity of the wind.

"Ed," came a disembodied voice, "Ed," "Ed," Ed," from all directions. Though, no one was there, and no one was speaking. Still, he forged on, determined and steadfast in his goal

Sensing a shift in the atmosphere, Ed dodged between two larger cars, hoping the wind would pass him by, that it wouldn't notice him cowering there in the shade. *It's just wind. Just rough wind.* In his heart, he knew this was something more. There was no explanation for Ginger's death. Still, he hoped the shelter from the cars would keep him safe until the gusts relented enough for him to move again. Part of him knew that's not how the wind worked, but a more significant part of him held on to that last shred of hope.

In the next few moments, he was smashed back against one of the vehicles, his old bones useless beneath the immense force. Ed's fingers bowed outward, bending and snapping at each joint; his fingers were broken backward. Ed screamed, looking down at his dangling fingers, tears streaming down his face. "No, no, I need to get home! I need to find my family! They need me!"

The wind began to pluck the nails from each of Ed's fingers, sucking them loose one by one as he writhed on the concrete—needless pain. Ed screamed again; the tips of his fingers were alight in white hot agony followed by throbbing and stinging. Delicately, the wind danced around Ed, a spiral of debris swirling into a deadly cyclone.

Ed, now sitting slumped between the two cars, felt a hard tug at his trousers. "What the hell? Stop!"

The tugging became insistent and painful, but thankfully, the fabric began to give way, splitting at the seam and ripping down between his legs. Eventually, the denim slipped free from his body, leaving his dick and balls exposed to the cold wind and slapping air. He'd discarded his underwear weeks ago once they'd reached the point of no return. Having had a dutiful wife, Ed had no idea how to clean his own clothes, and he was too prideful to ask any of the younger bar residents to help him.

He never expected to have spent so much time in the bar, and his pants too stunk of sweat and semen. He reached down, attempting to cover his manhood with his flopping, wrecked hands. His arms still worked. So, he was able to do a half-decent job of hiding his nether regions. But the wind picked up, swirling around his dick, his greasy pubic hairs pulling the skin of his pelvis taught, while his flaccid penis undulated back and forth like a dashboard hula girl. It may have been almost pleasurable in another situation, but this was just a horror show. The wind pulled and pulled until, finally, it gave a tremendous yank, ripping Ed's dick free from his body and then dropping it back down on top of his head with a wet plop. It rolled down his face leaving a trail of blood in its wake, smacking him on the nose and almost slipping into his open mouth.

Ed didn't have it in him to scream again as his severed dick caught on the collar of his shirt, laying their useless and wasted and draining fluids onto the filthy material. So, he sobbed quietly there against those cars, crying at his short-sightedness, crying because he'd done this to himself by forcing his way outside, and crying because he knew this was the end, that he'd never see his family again.

Blood ran freely from the gash where his penis had been moments ago, a hot stream of thick red gore splattering against the oil-stained concrete. His death wasn't quick. In his final moments, he thought starvation may have been the kinder way out.

Chapter Eleven: Earlier on Day One

Frieda, Athena, and Madison, three sisters ranging from their mid-thirties to their mid-forties, dressed in leggings and oversized t-shirts, were out for their daily power walk. They'd meet after work, Monday through Friday, to walk through town, drooling as they passed the various eateries and specialty shops but persevering as they all suffered from somewhat crippling body image issues.

The sisters, though not always in agreement, took this time to 'bitch and bond,' as they called it, and no topic was off limits. They'd even complain about one another when necessary, favoring directness and aggression when at odds. It wasn't the healthiest relationship, but they'd band together when necessary, like when they passed the wild red-headed woman headed to one of the town bars.

"Get out of my way, you cows," the woman spat. "Some of us want to get to happy hour, not look at your cottage cheese asses in those leggings."

Frieda, the eldest, stopped and turned toward the woman. "Excuse me? What did you just say to us?"

"You heard me, soccer mom. Move your fat disgusting ass out of my damn way. You cows are taking up the entire sidewalk."

"Oh, I don't think so," Frieda began, "I am not about to take crap from a skeevy alcoholic in the middle of the day. I don't have the patience for your assholery."

"Girlie, if you don't move, I'm going to knock you the fuck out." The woman closed her knobby hands into fists, curling her thumb on the outside of her fingers.

Athena—who'd had to bail her sister out of jail before—stepped in. "Look, lady, you can apologize to my sister here and go on your merry way, or you can deal with both of us."

The woman looked them up and down, laughing at the prospect. "This is America. You can't make me do anything. I am allowed to say whatever I damn well please. It's called free speech." She smiled, crossing her arms over her chest, looking indignant.

Madison, the wily one, casually stepped aside and walked around behind the woman, grabbing her by her orange cigarette-scented hair. "How many times do we need to do this, Ginger? You're always out here running your mouth about bullshit. I'm so tired of hearing it."

"How do you know my name?" Ginger spat, thrashing about, trying to free herself from the girl's grip.

"Bitch, you're drunk and stumbling around here yelling about 'Murica at least once a week. Everyone knows who you are: a pathetic, sad, awful drunk of a woman. You're mean and worthless. Everyone knows who you are, and everyone avoids your dumb ass."

Irate, Ginger doubled down on her efforts to get away from the girl, ripping hairs from her head in the process but not gaining her freedom. The two other sisters closed in on her, happy Madison had taken action.

"Now, who's got the upper hand?" Frieda asked, looking around cluelessly in an attempt to mock the angry woman in front of her. "Oh, I think it's us!" She smiled back at the awful woman.

Athena clapped. "It seems so, sisters. It seems so. Now, Ginger, is it? Are you planning to apologize, or do we have to beat the shit out of you? I wasn't looking to ruin my manicure today, but I can make a special exception just for you."

Ginger relented. "Fine. I'm sorry. Now, let me go before I start screaming for help."

Madison pulled tighter. "I don't think you're going to do that." Ginger locked eyes with Madison, promising silent revenge, before Madison loosed her grip and let Ginger free. "Once they saw it was you screaming, no one would come to help."

Ginger stumbled, losing her balance in the release, before looking back at the sisters and yelling, "Fuck you!" and running down the sidewalk toward her bar of choice.

"That was fun," Madison said as the three women resumed their walk. Ginger wasn't their only issue; people didn't much love the sisters; they were relics of the mean girl era that went out of fashion years ago.

While most people outgrow that stage of life, heading off to college or into the job market and building fully formed adult lives with adult responsibilities and adult problems, Frieda, Athena, and Madison had not. They'd all attended the local college, and they all, inexplicably, graduated with degrees in puppetry; they'd never really left their hometown. They never ventured out into the world or exposed themselves to other people from other cultures with different viewpoints or ideologies. Instead, they nourished their need to mock and look down on people around them, desiring control over everyone who dared set foot in their lives.

As they walked, feeling the air chill around them, the women quickened their steps.

"It's getting pretty windy out here," Athena remarked. "I think we should double-time it home to get out of this weather."

Frieda and Madison nodded before picking up the pace.

They were only about a half mile from Frieda's home, which is where all of their silver Priuses sat.

With each step, the wind grew harsher, blowing into their eyes, making it difficult to see, and whipping them against one another so they looked drunk and disorderly as they attempted their quick-paced walking.

"Yeesh. This is bizarre," Frieda began, holding her hand before her face to block the wind. "Was there even supposed to be a storm today?"

Athena attempted to grab her phone out of the tight spandex pocket of her favorite leggings, but as soon as she had it in her grasp, the wind took it, and it fell to the ground, shattered and useless. "Shit!" she yelled. "Predicted or not, it's certainly here, and we need to get indoors and now I need to get a new phone, too! Dammit!"

Frieda and Madison, growing increasingly leery, tried and failed to break into a run. To passersby, they probably looked like little kids attempting to run the wrong way up or down an escalator, making little to no progress as they pumped their middle-aged legs. Had they been watching others attempt such a feat, they'd have been a cackling mess of happy tears.

Yelling now over the sound of the ripping wind, Athena called to her sisters, "What do we do? I can't make any headway!"

Frieda and Madison, on the verge of tears, looked at one another and began screaming for help. Concentrated wind, more potent than any recorded tornado, entered their mouths and sinuses, ripping into their tissue as the harsh air was forced down their throats into their organs. Lungs punctured, the atmosphere made its way out into their bloodstreams as the sisters rasped, unable to take in a breath.

Athena watched in horror, beyond reach of either sister, as they raked at their respective throats and fell to the concrete. Within moments, the sisters were convulsing as air bubbles permeated their bloodstreams, shooting to their brain and heart, respectively, causing an aneurysm and heart attack. Frieda was the first to still, her arteries rupturing and spilling blood into her brain. Madison's death was prolonged by a slow dance between her ruptured lung and her blocked heart. The sisters were frozen in grotesque, unnatural final formulations, cooling there on the sidewalk while their remaining sister looked on helpless and terrified.

With both sisters dead, Athena cried, gut-wrenching sobs filling the air around her, feeding the wind her grief. The wind relented, giving the woman the freedom to move. When she realized she was no longer rooted to the spot, Athena dashed forward toward her broken sisters. She checked both for a pulse, wanting to make sure they were genuinely dead before breaking into a run. Finding none, she murmured an "I'm sorry" before making a run for it. Frieda's home was mere blocks away, and Athena was confident that if she could get to her Prius, she'd be able to fight the wind enough to go find some help somewhere, the police station, maybe. She'd at least be able to use a phone to call someone for help or support.

As the silver cars came into view, Athena felt a swell in her heart. She wrestled her key fob free, unlocking the car as she closed in. Her breaths coming hard, Athena gasped for air; a mix of adrenaline and fear and the physical toll running had taken on her body had her lungs burning and in need of an oxygen injection. With a stitch in her side, she grabbed for the car door, opening it. As she stepped toward her Prius, the wind flared up once again, slamming the door on her body, pinning her between the car's metal frame and the door itself.

Athena struggled, crying out for help, and the wind responded in kind, ebbing again so the door relaxed and Athena could attempt to move her painful body out of the snapping car door trap. But, in a second, the wind picked up again, slamming the door on her injured body anew. Over and over, the wind would release and resurge, hitting the bedraggled woman time and time again until she began to bleed internally. Her skin was perforated and bleeding in places as deep bruises started to bloom across parts of her mangled body. Eventually, hanging like a ragdoll from the half-closed door of her precious EV, Thick drool oozed from Athena's dead mouth as her half severed corpse leaked vital fluids onto the asphalt. Bones jutted from her mangled torso and bits of intestines bulged from her gashes and viscera seeped through her various wounds.

Chapter Twelve

Jade, Ryan, Micah, Liza, and Jorge sat huddled together, chatting about their predicament like they had several times before. The mood, sour and more urgent than usual, had taken a turn when Ed left and had grown worse because Ed hadn't returned. They assumed he hadn't survived. He'd have made good on his promise, of that they had no doubt. The man, for all his faults and proclivities, was a good person. In their own ways, the group had silently mourned his loss.

They sat waiting and hoping for good news. When none came and another two weeks went by, the group needed to get serious about what to do. Jade and Ryan moved Ginger's body to the other, now empty, freezer, freeing up their last food stores. The extra inventory from Ginger's freezer had extended their ability to stay in the bar by several weeks, and they could probably last a couple more as long as they limited food intake to a small breakfast and a meager dinner. It wasn't an ideal situation, but it was enough to sustain their lives just a little longer. Beer added to their caloric intake, and the sugar in the alcohol helped to keep them afloat. The beer itself could sustain them for a while, but they assumed it'd eventually kill them, too.

"We are going to have to leave at some point," Liza said, pragmatic but afraid. "I'm not eating Ginger. I'm just not, but I don't want to starve either."

"So, I think we all know that. We can't stay here forever, not with supplies running low, but what do we want to do when we leave?" Jade

113

asked.

Ryan, having thought it through. "The way I see it, we can do one of two things. Option A: someone, or maybe a few of us, go out to gather supplies from nearby businesses and then hurry back here. That extends our time and minimizes our risk, I think? Since we never heard Ed scream, he must have gotten far enough away from the building before anything happened to him. There are stores, bars, and restaurants all up and down the block. If there's no one else around, we can loot those places and bring our findings back here. If we fill up the freezers again, we will buy ourselves more time. That could keep us safe until some help arrives, hopefully arrives. Option B: we go out and try to find help. That'll probably mean we need cars of some kind. So, we should figure out who's parked closest. It's probably best to go in pairs so we can, maybe, look out for one another. I don't think anyone else should leave on their own. There's safety in numbers."

Micah scoffed. "We get it, you're the leader now, but those ideas are dumb."

"Do you have anything better? I sure don't. But we're all ears. So, if you've got something to propose, please do," Ryan said, his tone annoyed.

"No, I don't have another idea, but I remember what the wind did to that awful woman. It wasn't normal. Some kind of supernatural nonsense is going on, and it doesn't have to follow the rules. So, how can we even protect one another? How do you fight the wind?"

Ryan cursed his inability to learn physical geography. It was the most boring of the sciences, and he could barely stay awake in class. Scraping by with a D was all he was able to muster in college, and he was only required to take one undergraduate course. He didn't have a ton of wind knowledge packed into his head. He knew there was a way to dispel wind, at least temporarily, but he couldn't remember what. "I don't know, Micah, but that's the best I can come up with, okay?" Ryan looked out to the rest of the group. "Does anyone else have ideas?"

No one spoke.

"Okay, well, do we want to vote on an idea? I am not going to be responsible for everyone's fate. This needs to be a team decision."

They went back and forth before relenting, knowing Ed was inevitably correct that they needed to get out of the bar in order to find help.

"Okay, that's settled then. We're going out to find help," Ryan stated firmly. "We should probably make sure we have a solid plan. So, why don't we strategize over dinner tonight."

"I don't want to leave," Jade said. "This is my

place, and I am not going to abandon it. Plus, if we all go, who's going to make the Nine-one-one calls? I'm the odd one out, anyway. You folks came in pairs, and you can go searching in pairs. I'm going to hold down the fort. If things look dangerous, turn around. Come back, and I'll let you in. We have time to try things more than once. So, if things feel dangerous, get back here. We do have enough food for a couple more weeks. This isn't urgent."

Nervously, Ryan ran a hand through his dirty hair. He didn't want to leave Jade behind or at all, but he understood her rationale. "Are you sure? Do you want to stay here alone? I'd feel better if you came with us, but I understand if you can't. I just want to make sure this is what you really want."

"I would prefer not to be alone, but I can be. If someone's going to stay, it's going to be me. This is my ship, and I'll hold her as long as I can. I want to make sure the four of you have somewhere to run back to if you need an escape." She smiled, the expression was like a promise.

"Okay, then. Do we maybe want to have two groups? We can split up, and half of us can look for resources to bring back to the bar, and the other half can find a car and go in search of help?"

"Yes," Liza said, "that makes sense. Jorge and I can gather supplies. The three of us will wait for the cavalry once we're back. Extra food will buy us all a little more time. So, you won't need to rush back immediately."

Ryan looked over to Micah, wondering if he'd be a reliable partner. "Micah? That okay with you? Can we head for some help?"

"Yeah, whatever, fine," he replied. "So, when are we doing this thing?"

After some debate, they all agreed to leave the following day. They ate one more dinner as a group, this one a little larger than they'd been having, to raise their spirits and their stamina.

"That was great, Jade. Thank you," Jorge offered, "Let me do the dishes tonight, okay?"

"No," Jade said. "Leave them. I can do them tomorrow. It'll keep me distracted for a while."

When it came time to sleep, Liza and Jorge pushed the comfy chairs together, settling in next to one another, their hands entwined in a sibling embrace. Micah, annoyed that he didn't get a comfy spot on his last night, decided to use some bar rags as a pillow and settled in on the pool table. The older man was gone, and he may as well make use of the table. He could at least stretch out there.

Ryan and Jade, no longer sneaking around, made their way back to her office for one last screw before falling asleep uncomfortably tangled on the office's loveseat.

In the morning, they slowly moved everything away from the front door, and Jade handed a key to Liza so she could get back in once they'd gathered supplies. "Just in case I can't hear you or can't get to the door fast enough. Let yourself back in. I won't barricade the door too much. So, you two just push extra hard if you need to. Okay?"

Liza nodded in reply. "We won't be gone long."

Jade took a deep breath, looking around the bar, wistfully as if gauging being left alone forever; a single tear rolled down her cheek as she gazed on at the group. She lingered longer on Ryan, meeting his eyes for a brief but intense moment. "And you two, please find a way to communicate as soon as you can. Hell, drop off a walkie-talkie if it comes down to it. I will be a mess worrying about you both."

Micah rolled his eyes.

"Of course. We won't stay away a minute longer than we need to. As soon as we find help or get word to someone, we will head back."

If some or all of them made it, they would come back for her.

"Really, we'll be back for you, Jade," Ryan promised, pressing a wet kiss to her worried lips. "As soon as we find or learn what we need to, I'll be knocking on that damn door. You have my

118

word."

The group of four, huddled together, opened the door and stepped out into the world, shutting the door firmly behind them. Liza patted her pocket to make sure the key was there and that she'd be able to get back in. They heard the hard metallic click of Jade locking up shop one more time.

—

I been waiting. Hungry. Starving. My hollow wails crying out, ready to consume the essence of humanities last vestiges. And, so they've given in, their own hunger taking precedent. Weak human bodies. With a laugh and a flourish, I gathered my breath, violently rotating columns of air, readying myself for more delicious flesh-covered souls.

—

The winds were heavy, mad even, seeming much worse than they'd been when Ed stepped out into the street. The four of them stumbled, being pressed together by the suffocating wind. No one was able to take a single step in any direction.

The winds wrapped around them like an invisible rope, squishing them closer together. Back to back to back to back. Reaching out, the motley group clasped hands, creating a sense of solidarity.

"I think we made a mistake. We shouldn't have all gone out together like this," Liza began. "This awful wind was waiting for us. We never had a chance."

"It's not over yet, Liza. You can't think like that," Jorge called. "We can do this. We just need to push back."

Trash and stray bits of nature swirled at their feet, nipping at them, softly but with increasing fury as the winds picked up. The town remained desolate, save the rotting bodies still littering the street and broken storefronts. Liza looked to her brother, eyes wide with fear, but he smiled back at her with youthful confidence and kindness. Micah groaned as he strained against the wind, attempting to press his way out and back to the bar, but gaining no headway. Only Ryan remained steadfast in his goal. He pushed his foot forward one millimeter at a time, determined to break free, to get somewhere, to find help.

The wind picked up, stronger than before, stronger than either Micah or Ryan had witnessed. It pressed them closer together as if they were being lassoed and roped. Pressure built against their skin causing their limbs to bend at awkward angles as they stood there rounded up with no escape.

Try as they might, no amount of effort freed them from the little cluster they'd been forced into. "I told you," Micah piped in. "I told you this wasn't going to work. Why does no one ever listen to me? And what do I get for going along with your stupid plan? Death. That's what I get. Stupid senseless death."

"I get that this isn't ideal but tone down the sass. We've got to come up with a plan of action instead of whining like babies," Ryan spat.

"Plan? What plan?" Micah asked, a note of incredulity present in his voice. He used his eyes to gesture towards the town.

More and more debris began to accumulate, sucked in by the wind and hurled right at the group. Stray nails and bobby pins smacked their skin leaving hard red welts. The wind whipped their skin. leaving red burns on their faces and hands. A large wrench clunked Jorge in the mouth, knocking a few teeth out in the process. His teeth spilled from his gaping maw and fell into the wind, useless to him, and lost forever as blood poured over his lips and splashed back onto his face.

"I wasn't trying to be a dick," Micah said, which did nothing to soothe the panicked group.

"I get that our skip day sort of went off the rails, and maybe you blame me for that. I'm sorry if you do..."

"Are you really that dumb, Ryan? You don't know why I've been acting this way?"

Liza looked over to her brother as he winced in

pain, but still he eyed her kindly and attempted another more gummy smile. Ryan, with great effort, turned his head just enough to look Micah in the eyes.

"No, why would I?" Ryan replied, bewildered by the question.

"Jade," Micah said, finally getting his little secret off his chest.

"Jade? You have a thing for her? I didn't know, man. You never said anything. I didn't plan things this way."

Micah's mouth hung open. "No, you idiot. I wasn't into her! I was into you!"

At his confession, Micah was struck in the forehead by a wayward branch which left a deep cut across his face. He screamed, pain welling up, but held Ryan's gaze.

"Are you okay? Wait, what? You're gay?" Ryan said as the scent of decay crept its way into his nostrils.

"Of course I'm gay! I'm a flamboyant art teacher. Was that not enough of a hint? What about all of the flirting we used to do? You didn't know then?"

"What flirting?" Indeed, at a loss, Ryan didn't know what to say. He'd always been bad at that sort of thing, believing people were just overly nice and not that they were interested in him. He didn't think he was that much of a catch and assumed others didn't either.

"I flirt with you most days! You've really never noticed?"

"No, sorry, man. I really had no idea." If he could have shrugged, he would have, but the tension from the wind held him in place with very little wiggle room. "I am not good at picking up on signals."

"It's great that you two are working shit out," Liza interjected, "but what the hell do we do now?" She tried to wriggle free. She pushed with all her strength, but there was no slack in the wind's grip.

The wind stopped. Entirely. And the group fell to the ground, skinning palms and knees as they fell towards the concrete with extreme force.

"Run!" Ryan yelled.

Liza was off in a moments notice, grabbing her brother's hand and dragging him down the street away from the bar and towards her car. Micah, zonked from having hit the ground with such force, and bleeding freely from his head wound, was slower to move. Ryan rushed over to help his friend despite their current situation.

"Come on. We have to go."

"Huh?" Micah said, as Ryan yanked on his arm, willing him to get up and moving.

The wind began to build again, slowly at first,

but menacing and strong within seconds. Micah and Ryan were picked up, in the grip of an invisible force, and placed back down in front of the bar. Rooted to the spot again, they were stuck with no hope of escape. Liza's scream carried across the wind and back to the wayward professors.

"Shit," Ryan said.

The wind had hold of the brother sister duo as well. They were being pushed backwards on the sidewalk, shoes skidding, soles burning. Both flailed wildly, fighting to regain momentum, but neither was a match for the wind. It picked them up with ease and brought them back to the bar's gateway as well. Hovering above the ground, Liza cried out while Jorge yelled at her to remain strong, not to worry, that they'd find a way out, that they'd laugh about this one day. They dangled above the ground as the wind jostled them about like human marionettes. Jorge did his best to remain strong for Liza, but the wind had him in a vice-like grip and his neck snapped right there in the air, all life going out of his young body.

Liza screamed as she was tossed to the ground with Micah and Ryan. An in visible rope of wind tightened around them, squeezing with more force as the seconds passed. Liza's bones began to crack. Her arms and legs, breaking under the pressure, white bones sticking out haphazardly through her now torn flesh. Air was ripped from the group's lungs as the vacuum around them sucked away what precious gasps they were able to inhale while being squeezed to death.

Micah cast a wanting glance back at the door to the bar. They'd barely meandered out onto the sidewalk. Safety was so close, but still unattainable. Three feet more and they'd be able to get back to Jade, to the sturdy bar where they could last just a while longer. Though, no one had the medical skills to tend to Liza's copious injuries and she was bleeding heavily, red stains blooming across her haggard clothing. The key to the bar was still nestled safely in her pocket, but it was useless to all of them. No one could reach they key. No one could get to the door, even though it was a mere three feet away.

"Maybe we can push together?" Ryan offered, his last ditch attempt at surviving. His breaths were coming in shallow gasps and each inhale felt like a stab to the chest. The pressure from the wind and a likely broken rib was keeping his chest from fully inflating.

Try as they might, they couldn't budge an inch. It was useless. The wind was too strong. Even in top form, none of them were a match for it.

"This is it," Micah began, "we're toast."

With that, the wind pressed in further,

flattening each member of their motley crew, like freshly ironed laundry. Liza was gone before the worst of it, succumbed to her injuries. In the end, that was a kindness. Micah looked over to Ryan who was looking his way, seeing him for everything he was and wasn't.

With a final gurgle, Micah's organs began squeezing up his trachea, into his mouth, and outward, one-by-one. He didn't even have a chance to scream before being turned into a human toothpaste tube, dispensing organs, blood, and viscera down his chest and onto the concrete below.

Ryan gagged at the grotesque sight in front of him before he ran out of air. Foam and mucus dripped from his mouth as his heart slowed and stilled. His wide unseeing eyes filled with red splatters as did his face and neck, purple splotches marring his once clear skin. The group fell dead, mangled, into a discarded pile right at Jade's doorstep.

As the first two days passed, their corpses began to decompose like the rest of the bodies in town. Discolored and dead, stiff from rigor mortis, they bloated, the stench of their carcasses carried through the streets by the devastating wind, permeating the air, staining the environment with its wretched scent.

—

By day three, Jade's hope had all but faded. She found it incredibly hard to pass the time on her own, and she was devastated at the prospect of losing Ryan for good. *I shouldn't have let him leave. Why didn't I try harder to stop him, to stop them? They could have gone two by two instead of all at once. This was a shit plan.*

Once a week had passed, Jade felt empty. She still tried 911 every day, once an hour instead of once every half hour, and her calls always resulted the same way, with an empty *ring, ring, ring,* and no answer.

Jade knew no one was coming back. She now believed the wind wouldn't leave until it had claimed every life. So, the strong neon light from the bar was like a slap in the face for the raging entity.

—

Others had survived beyond the initial storm, but time had claimed their lives, too. The educator orgy group, deciding to spend the remainder of their days rutting away and indulging in carnal desires, eventually starved to death in that auditorium, dying in a sweaty pile of naked and satiated flesh, the burnt stench of coffee beans covered their stink, but only for a time...

Malaysia, Benetto, and Annette had found solace in the fallout shelter. They had water and dried food rations, but when stores ran low, Benetto bashed his two female companion's heads in with a large rock so that he could survive a while longer, and when the food ran out, he made his way up to the surface again where the wind was waiting to tear his flesh away like the others who'd met their ends trying to escape the building. His skin was stretched thin and ripped from his body, and he died screaming while attempting to hold his entrails cradled in his sinewy arms.

The boy in the ice cream shop lasted the longest, slowly making his way through the different flavors of ice cream and various cones and toppings. He'd darted beneath a table when he saw an old man struggling outside. After having not seen a living person in several weeks, he distrusted the man. Instead of calling out to him, he decided to hide instead. He thought he'd be able to ride this thing out until it was over or until some kind of military help showed up or something. Unfortunately for him, the only person who showed up was a little girl with a big sharp knife. She'd introduced herself as Mary, tapping at the window wide-eyed and demure and asking for help. While the boy had hidden from the old man, he couldn't leave a young child out there to fend for herself, a mistake on his part. She'd stabbed him while he slept, perched on his chest and peering into his terrified eyes until his heart stilled and he could no longer see.

Mary was immune to the wind, her dark companion. It allowed her to roam freely to create her own chaos. Happy with her new digs, Mary tucked into the remaining ice cream tubs. While most were about ⅔ empty, she pried the lid off one in a back freezer and found it full and only slightly freezer-burned. She reached in to pull the giant tub out after finding a suitable spoon, and she dug in, scooping large globs of chocolatey marshmallow ice cream into her wanting mouth. After minutes, she felt off, hot, and itchy. Panicked, she reached for the top of the ice cream tub and turned it over to look at the ice cream's label: Non-dairy, almond milk, rocky road.

"Oh, no," she exclaimed, "almonds!" as she scratched at her swelling throat and eyes. Without an epi-pen or a doctor's intervention, she wasn't long for the world, and she died gasping and red.

Epilogue

In the emergency station, the outpost just outside of town, the purple corpse of the on-duty dispatch officer sat slumped over, face buried into her spilt Slurpee. The icy beverage had long since melted, leaving a puddle of sticky blue liquid dripping onto the dispatcher's pressed khaki uniform pants and onto the floor.

The station's phone lit up, *ring, ring, ring,* though there was no one left to answer the call. All of those calls, *ring, ring, ring,* desperate folks, the unlucky ones who'd escaped the wind's initial machinations, doing the one thing they'd been taught to do since childhood. Dial 911. Get help.

As the days passed, the calls slowed, *ring, ring, ring,* as folks ventured out into the howling derecho. Siloed, no one knew what to expect or how far the wind extended. The television stations went to just static after a few days, and the internet had ceased working almost immediately. So, most folks were clueless, thinking they'd fallen victim to a particularly terrible windstorm, one for the ages even.

By the time they realized the reality of their situation, their skin was burning away or they were caught vice-like in its grip, organs squeezed up from their stomachs and out their wrecked throats. The hungry wind had no method to its madness; it just wanted to feed, to snuff out life, to silence the landscape in its path.

The more intelligent folks, or the ones who'd glimpsed the improbable mad wind, stayed inside the longest. But when food stores ran out and they weren't willing to eat one another (though some were), the only choices left were suicide or excruciating death by wind. While many had hope, it was ill-placed. There was no hope, not anymore, not here.

Jade was the final holdout, and she held on as long as she could, but lacking food, she couldn't last forever. Hallucinating and half-mad, she clung to the idea that Ryan or Liza or Jorge would return. She'd have even been thrilled if Micah showed up. But they didn't, and her little ember of hope dried and cracked with time. Her call was the last, an afternoon *ring, ring, ring,* her final listless attempt at reaching emergency services. Eventually, when no one returned for her, she decided she'd end her life on her own terms. Rigging a noose made of duct tape and bar towels up on one of the metal ceiling beams, Jade affixed the makeshift rope to her neck and jumped down off the bar, hanging herself.

—

Feeling robbed of a final kill but knowing Earth no longer held life for them to take, the winds calmed, disappearing back into the dimensional gash through which they'd entered, still hungry and in search of new life to steal. The winds were attracted to imperfect life, the kind that had fractured somewhere along the timeline. They ached for depravity but loved the sweet taste of innocence as well. Earth had been a buffet, one that it had sucked dry, one that it was almost sad to leave. But there would be more life to steal, more places to terrorize, and that delighted the wind.

—

With calls no longer coming in, the station's lights clicked off, shrouding the dispatcher's bloated corpse in darkness, left alone to deteriorate with a modicum of dignity.

—

With the devouring of these souls, empty carcasses tossed about and rotting, there was nothing left to sate my empty spaces. No souls to feed my endless hunger. Their lives filled my void for days, warm moments of bliss, but this place holds nothing for me now. There are other places to destroy, to consume, and I'll enjoy a new torture, more screams. Yes. I think I'll enjoy that very much.